Henk,

Thanks for everything

Mike Price.

The author was born in 1941 in Bidford-on-Avon. He has lived in Coventry all his life. Educated at John Gulson Grammar School and then at Lanchester Polytechnic, studying Building Management, he went into business at the age of 24, successfully taking one company to the stock market.

He is married to his second wife and has a son and daughter from his first marriage. Mike Price is now semi-retired.

The Lost Father

To
'Noreen Steere' – My mother

Mike Price

The Lost Father

Vanguard Press

VANGUARD PAPERBACK

© Copyright 2011
Mike Price

The right of Mike Price to be identified as author of
this work has been asserted by him in accordance with the
Copyright, Designs and Patents Act 1988.

All Rights Reserved

No reproduction, copy or transmission of this publication
may be made without written permission.
No paragraph of this publication may be reproduced,
copied or transmitted save with the written permission of the publisher,
or in accordance with the provisions
of the Copyright Act 1956 (as amended).

Any person who commits any unauthorised act in relation to
this publication may be liable to criminal
prosecution and civil claims for damages.

All names and events in this novel are fictitious and bear no
resemblance to any person living or dead.

A CIP catalogue record for this title is
available from the British Library.

ISBN 978 1 84386 707 4

*Vanguard Press is an imprint of
Pegasus Elliot MacKenzie Publishers Ltd.*
www.pegasuspublishers.com

First Published in 2011

**Vanguard Press
Sheraton House Castle Park
Cambridge England**

Printed & Bound in Great Britain

Acknowledgements

With thanks to all my friends who read the first drafts and encouraged me with their comments and a very special thanks to my wife, Marie, who has supported my efforts and is my rock.

CHAPTER ONE

The ambulance screeched to a halt in front of the burning building. Isabel jumped down from the cab, cigarette dangling from the corner of her mouth, her eyes dark with fatigue. It was eight thirty and she had been on the go almost constantly for thirteen hours. The stench of death reached her nostrils as the medics tried in vain to find signs of life in any of the bodies that lay on the pavement.

They ought to change her job description from ambulance driver to body collector. She always seemed to arrive to clear up the mess, not save anyone. The bomb had landed on top of the house, blowing out the upstairs walls and windows causing the remains of the roof to collapse onto the ground floor. Those who didn't die from the blast were crushed by the masonry and timber.

A family of four, the mother and her children, two young boys and a teenage girl had died, hopefully instantly.

Isabel didn't cry anymore, death was an ever present fact of life.

The firemen had managed to get the blaze under control now and the only task for her and her two man crew was to get the bodies back to the mortuary. If the family's father survived the war he would come home to find he had nothing. What was the point of it all?

It was November 1940 and the worst of the blitz was raining down on Coventry. Isabel was only twenty but looked older. She had seen sights that would live with her for the rest of her life. It had made her cold and emotionless, frightened to make friends or have any meaningful relationships, in case they would be stolen from her like her father had been. He had been one of the first to be called up; having served as a major in the first war he'd been on the reserve list. He had survived that war and even been decorated for his bravery, but his luck ran out in the fiasco that was Dunkirk, dying on the beaches waiting for a boat to get him back home. The Luftwaffe had swept down shooting them like fish in a barrel, they never had a chance. It was the death of her father that had prompted her to volunteer to drive for the ambulance service.

Back at the ambulance station she parked and locked the doors of the cab. It was time for the next shift to take over. There was no respite. The constant drone of planes flying low over the city with their cargo of death could be heard interrupted by the wail of the air raid sirens. She lit another Park Drive, the second packet of the day was nearly empty, but the cigarettes and the coffee were what kept her going. She walked to the locker room and took off her overalls and the scarf that held her hair in place. Putting on her white blouse, dark slacks and high heeled shoes, she felt more like a woman. The transformation was completed by the application of bright red lipstick. Her hair was long and had natural soft curls that now cascaded down her back, free of the binding that the scarf had been. She wrapped herself in a woollen jumper that her mother had knitted for her and then pulled on her thick overcoat. She was ready for the cold air that hit her as she left the building.

Isabel was attractive but not beautiful, her eyes were dark brown and when she smiled her face lit up, but sadly she smiled rarely these days. The feature that stopped her being beautiful was her nose. It had broken when she ran into another girl at school and it had set at a slight angle. She was more conscious of her nose than anyone else ever seemed to be; but a broken nose was nothing compared with the suffering that was all around her.

Isabel lived with her mother in Coundon, which was only a mile from the ambulance station, so walked home at the end of each shift. The Germans were concentrating their raids onto the factories which had been converted to provide munitions for the war effort, but often they were off target and that was when the estates nearby took the brunt of the bombing.

As usual, her mother was in the kitchen trying to conjure up something wholesome to eat on the meagre rations that they had.

The wireless was sitting on the kitchen table churning out more depressing news by the minute.

The house was cold; her mother never lit a fire until she had to. Isabel went into the living room and taking some sheets of an old newspaper, kneeled on the floor and began rolling the paper into spills which she then folded on themselves to form crude firelighters. When she had produced eight, she arranged them in the hearth and added some wood that lay on top of the coal scuttle. She lit the spills and once the wood had started to burn placed a few lumps of coal on top. The fire burst into life and the room took on a glow from the reflections of the flames.

Isabel still kept her jumper on; it would take some time before the fire warmed the room enough to dispense with it.

The routine was the same every week night. She and her mother would sit at the table and eat their dinner hardly speaking. Isabel would clear the dishes away then make her mother a cup of tea, which she drank whilst Isabel washed up. Isabel would bring the radio in from the kitchen and set the station to the light programme and her mother would settle down with her knitting to listen, non stop until she went to bed. Her mother was for ever knitting; jumpers, scarves, socks for neighbours' children anything that could be made she would turn her hand to.

Isabel lit a cigarette and opened her book. The noise of the radio in the background never bothered her; it was like the chimes of a grandfather clock, after a while you forgot all about them.

Weekends were different for Isabel if not for her mother. Since the death of her husband her mother had retreated into her shell, as though she was trying to wrap herself in some invisible cocoon away from the horror of the war, waiting for it to be over so life could return to normality. However, it could never be normal again. Isabel was sure her mother believed that one day her father would return and they would wake up from this nightmare. Although she loved her mother she knew life had to go on. She was young and single and was going to enjoy herself in spite of everything and had made up her mind, like many others, that she would live for today and to hell with tomorrow.

On Saturday night there was always a dance on somewhere and Isabel with her friend Grace made sure they attended. This Saturday they had been told that upstairs in the Pilot, a local pub, the Jordan Swing Band were playing and they decided that would be this week's choice.

A loud rapping on the front door signalled Grace's arrival to collect her friend. Isabel beckoned her to come in and showed her through to the living room, where her mother was already well into her latest scarf. Although the house had two downstairs reception rooms, only one was ever used. The front room was kept for 'best' though what that meant no one knew. Grace said hello to Isabel's mother who she always referred to as Mrs Brown, never for one moment did she consider using her Christian name.

Grace pulled a chair from under the dining table and sat down watching, fascinated by the click-click of the needles as they sped through the wool. Isabel came down the stairs having finished putting on her make-up. Her mother did not approve of the amount she wore, but then, she was much older and even in her younger days had hardly bothered with make-up herself.

Isabel picked up her handbag and after making sure there was a fresh packet of cigarettes and her house keys in it, snapped it shut. She kissed her mother on the cheek and told her not to wait up. Stopping only to get their coats the two girls left for the short walk to the bus stop.

By the time they had taken one bus into the town, then changed to the number 2 out to the Pilot, the dance had already started. They checked their coats into the cloakroom and made their way to the bar.

"Two gin and oranges please." Isabel had forced her way to the front and had caught the barman's eye.

"Thanks Bel, I needed that," Grace said after almost emptying her glass in one gulp.

"Take it easy we've got all night you know," Isabel laughed, but they were here to have a good time.

They finished their drinks and were about to order another round when two young men in army uniforms came over to them.

"Hi! I'm Tommy and this is my mate, Mick, would you lovely ladies like a dance or are you just here to admire the view?"

Grace giggled, she loved attention and Tommy had not stopped looking at her since they came over.

"Shall we?" Mick held out his hand towards Isabel and she followed him onto the dance floor.

He was good. The majority of the men she had danced with had no rhythm and spent most of the dance either standing on her shoes or bumping into her, but not Mick, he was good. After three dances on the trot they came back to the bar where Grace was deep in conversation with Tommy.

"What would you like to drink?" Mick asked her.

"A gin and orange, please."

He called the barman over and ordered her drink and a pint for himself. He didn't bother to ask Tommy... he was busy!

Mick was good company: easy to talk to and unlike most of the men she had met, didn't just want to talk about himself. He and Tommy were on a forty-eight hour pass and had to be back at camp by 7.00 pm on Sunday. He could not tell her where he was going to be posted, not for any other reason than he didn't know himself, as he said: he was just a corporal and was one of the last to know anything! She liked his down-to-earth honesty and, in truth, didn't want to know where he was being sent. After all she probably wouldn't see him again. What they both wanted was to forget the horrors of the war, even if only for a few hours, and enjoy the moment. Mick seemed to sense her feelings and, finishing his drink, gently guided her back to the dance floor.

The evening passed all too quickly and before they knew it the compere was announcing the last waltz. Mick drew her close to him as they glided around the floor, oblivious to all the other couples around them. The music finally died and for a moment they stood where they were, locked in each other's arms in a world apart, away from reality. The spell was broken by Tommy saying it was time to go.

"Would you like a lift home?" Mick asked Isabel, "I think we can just about afford a cab between us."

He looked at Tommy to check that he agreed. Tommy nodded his approval. Isabel and Grace exchanged glances and Grace smiled. Nothing more was said, they would be going home by taxi.

The cab dropped Tommy and Grace off and then drove the two streets to where Isabel lived. Having paid the driver Mick looked at her, a half smile playing on his lips.

"You are going to invite me in for a drink aren't you?"

"Yes, I suppose so but you'll have to be quiet, I don't want my mother coming down and asking awkward questions."

She turned the key in the door and they went into the hall. Her mother had left a lamp on so there was no need to switch all the lights on. He followed her into the kitchen.

"Coffee or would you like something stronger?"

"Something stronger please, have you any whisky?"

She reached in the cupboard and withdrew two tumblers, then bending down, took a half empty bottle of Haig from the back of a cupboard that housed the flour and cereals.

"It's my mother's hiding place," she said in answer to his unspoken question.

She poured two generous helpings of whisky and added a similar quantity of water to her glass. He shook his head, putting his hand over his glass. He only drank Scotch neat; why dilute it?

They took their drinks into the front living room, the 'best room', and sat on the settee, the only illumination that of the glow from the hall lamp through the glass panes of the lounge door. Isabel cuddled close to him. The room was cold. No fire had been lit for at least three weeks, the last time visitors had called and been shown into the 'best room'.

Mick didn't mind the cold; he had suffered a lot worse and it was a good excuse to get close to her. They drank their whisky in silence.

The empty glasses stood side-by-side on the coffee table. Mick stroked her hair and drew her face towards his, gently kissing her on the lips. He felt her body pressed next to his as she kissed him hard, her tongue exploring his lips and mouth. Their kisses lasted longer and longer as one followed another.

His hand moved to her breast and she made no move to dissuade him. She was wearing a blouse and skirt and the buttons on her blouse popped undone with his expert touch. His hand slid into her bra and cupped her breast; her nipples were hard under his touch. All the time she never stopped kissing him. She slid down so that she was lying full length on the settee. His hand was now stroking her leg, sliding over the smooth stockings till he reached the top and the bare flesh of her thigh covered only by the thin straps of her suspender belt. There was no resistance. He could feel her body quiver with each touch as inch-by-inch he explored until his fingers felt the edge of her panties and on and on inside gently caressing. She groaned and with her hands behind his head pulled him tighter to her. He pulled away from her but only so that he could slide her panties down and undo his trousers.

"Please, please," she moaned.

He lay on top of her and pressed himself inside. She was wet and he took her, gently at first and then with a ferocity that was almost animalistic. Her fingernails dug into his back and even through the thick material of his shirt he could feel the pain, a beautiful pain, born of lust. They both climaxed, her first and then him, heightened by the ecstasy he could feel when she was at her peak.

There were no words of love, they both knew that this was not love; it was if anything more important, a need, like eating or breathing. There would be no recriminations, no inquest, no guilt.

"Any chance of another whiskey, it's thirsty work you know?" Mick smiled at her.

She smiled back. Pulling her knickers back on and buttoning her blouse, she got up and took the glasses to the kitchen. When she came back with the drinks, Mick was sitting fully dressed as though nothing had happened.

Half an hour later Mick left. She never saw him again.

CHAPTER TWO

Jayne looked up from the book she was reading and surveyed the room. Yes all her pupils had their heads down busily writing. It was nearly the end of term and she had given them last year's history GCE paper as a mock test. Next year they would be sitting the real thing and she wondered just how many would be good enough to be entered, let alone pass! A further ten minutes passed before the bell rang to signal the end of the period.

One by one they trooped forward to hand in their papers. Jayne collected them together and slid them into her briefcase. It was Friday and with no further classes to take that day she had decided to get away early. The papers could be marked over the weekend, right now all she wanted was to get home and put her feet up.

Jayne Harris was forty-one and had inherited her mother's dark brown eyes and curly hair. An attractive woman who was often taken for someone in their mid thirties, a comment that for some reason annoyed her two sons; she felt they should be proud that their mother looked young, not embarrassed. She had been a teacher since qualifying at teacher training college and had worked continuously except for time off for the birth of her two children. Jayne had married her childhood sweetheart at the frighteningly early age of nineteen whilst still at university, and had proved what everybody had warned, that she had been too young. After eleven years she had found out that Ron was not the adoring husband she thought she knew.

A burst main had forced the Head into shutting the school and sending all the pupils and staff home at lunch time. Jayne had pulled into her drive, surprised to find Ron's car there when he was supposed to be meeting a client in Manchester. Worried that he might be ill, she let herself into the house and went straight upstairs to check he was alright. He was indeed alright, in fact a picture of rude health. He was stark naked riding Tracy, her 'best friend', like a cowboy taming a bucking bronco!!

She smiled to herself as she remembered the incident that had happened twelve years ago. She could laugh now but at the time she was devastated. Ron had tried all manner of excuses to try and save his marriage; after all he was not in love with Tracy, 'just playing' as he so endearingly put it. Jayne was not to be moved and filed for divorce as soon as he had packed his bags.

The experience had put her off men for a long time. Her mother had tried to talk her round, explaining it was just life and she should get on with it, but then Jayne's mum had a different outlook on love and marriage. She had been married three times and none of her husbands had been Jayne's dad!

Jayne had been single ever since and although she had had a few relationships, none had ever materialised into anything serious. To be fair, every time it looked as though her latest boyfriend wanted to settle down she panicked and found a way to end it.

Her two boys were growing up. James was in his second year at university and Nigel was about to start at Loughborough studying sports science. From September onwards she would be on her own.

Since her divorce the boys had spent alternate weekends with their father, so she was used to her own company. Whenever she had a relationship she would only allow the boyfriend to stay with her when the boys were at their father's. She knew it was perhaps old-fashioned and no doubt James and Nigel knew what was going on, but she had set certain standards and had to maintain them. She certainly did not have her mother's free spirit.

Jayne arrived home, parked her car in the garage and picking up her briefcase from the passenger seat, locked the garage doors and let herself into the house. It was quiet, with only the sound of the hall clock breaking the silence. Nigel would be home from sixth form in about an hour, so she would have time for a cup of tea and catch up on the day's papers. She walked through to the kitchen and switched the kettle on. Within a couple of minutes it had boiled and armed with a steaming mug of tea, she settled down in the living room to read the day's news.

She woke with a start as Nigel called out that he was home. The mug of tea, half drunk, sat cold on the table beside her, the papers in a heap on the floor. Nigel smiled as he bent down and kissed her.

"It must have been a gruelling day at school," he said sarcastically, albeit in a teasing voice.

She did not rise to the bait, instead went through to the kitchen to make a fresh cup of tea. If she had a favourite, and of course she did not, then Nigel would have won the role. Where James looked more like his father, Nigel had his mother's hair colouring handed down from his grandmother.

Nigel would be eighteen on the first of July and Jayne had promised to take him, and whoever was the current girlfriend at the time, out to dinner to celebrate. What Nigel didn't know was that Jayne had arranged for James to be there and had even invited Ron, his dad, on condition he came alone! The party was still two weeks away but Jayne had to have everything organised well in advance. She was a stickler for detail to the point of being annoying at times.

Nigel had gone upstairs to his room as soon as he had arrived home and she assumed that he had homework that he wanted to complete straight away to leave the weekend free. She never needed to moan at Nigel to do his homework. He always knuckled down straight away, unlike James who she had to constantly nag to get him to finish his work, rather than leave it to the last minute. The boys were opposites except for the fact they were both bright. James found schoolwork easy whereas Nigel had to apply himself, but they both got there in their own way. Jayne was proud of them both and secretly pleased that, despite the breakdown in her marriage, the boys had come through it relatively unscathed. It was a surprise therefore when half an hour later Nigel came downstairs, washed, changed and ready to go out. Without waiting to be questioned he bent down, gave his mother a peck on the cheek and with a "Don't wait up" disappeared down the hall.

She sat motionless on the settee, slightly taken aback by her son's actions. It was out of character for Nigel, who was usually so considerate and always spent some time with her discussing the day's happenings; stranger still for him to go out without having dinner, unless of course he was dining out, but he always gave her plenty of notice.

She thought of all the possible scenarios that had led to his behaviour but no rational explanation came to mind. No doubt he would tell her in the fullness of time.

If Nigel was eating out then why shouldn't she?

She dialled Debra's number. Debra was also a divorcee and she and Jayne often went out together if neither had a current beau. The phone rang out several times and Jayne was about to give up when a breathless Debra finally answered. Jayne quickly explained Nigel's strange behaviour and asked if she was free and would she fancy a girly night out. The response was an enthusiastic yes.

Jayne was not a big drinker but felt strongly about drinking and driving so had arranged for a taxi to collect her and drop her at the Chinese restaurant that she had booked for them.

Debra was seated at the table when she arrived, a bottle of white wine uncorked and reduced by one glass already. The waiter took Jayne's coat and returned with a menu. The menus were superfluous, the girls always had the same thing when they ate Chinese. They started with 'House Platter' a selection of different starters and followed with Chicken Chow Mein. Neither were adventurous diners and Nigel was always berating his mother to try something different!

The waiter smiled as he took the order, he remembered the two women and now knew their order by heart.

Debra was eager to hear all about Nigel and what Jayne thought was going on.

"To be honest I think he must have a new girlfriend, I don't think there is any big mystery." Jayne really had no idea but did not want to let her friend know that.

The conversation soon moved away from the children and on to more important things... like men.

Debra had recently finished with her 'boyfriend' when she found out that he was married with a family in Weston-Super-Mare, whilst pretending to be a divorcee living in Coventry.

She had been upset at first, more about being duped than the actual break up. In truth the relationship had run its course and she had been wondering how to extricate herself without hurting him. She need not have worried! As she said to Jayne, the sex had been brilliant at first and there was no doubt that he had been a good lover, but as the weeks had gone by he had wanted to do things which were a little more than fun and games and she had drawn the line at water sports.

Neither had a man in their lives at the present time, and while this didn't bother Jayne particularly, Debra was a far more sexual being and needed the attention that came with a new flame though, truth to tell, the initial excitement never seemed to last very long.

The two friends finished their meal and settled the bill. Jayne asked the waiter if he would call them a taxi and they finished off the wine whilst they waited. The taxi arrived within ten minutes and half an hour later Jayne was unlocking her front door. There were no lights on which meant Nigel was still out. It was only eleven, he would be home soon.

Jayne walked through to the kitchen and switched the kettle on to make a cup of tea. The kettle soon boiled and she poured the hot water over the tea bag into her favourite mug. Having added a little milk she took the drink into the lounge and set it down on the table next to her armchair. She was not ready for bed yet and wanted to wind down before going up.

Nigel came into her thoughts, but only for a second. He was old enough now to look after himself and would not thank her for staying up on his account. No it was not Nigel she thought about on these occasions, when alone and quiet, it was her father. It was strange that these last two or three months she had started to think of the father she had never met or even known about.

CHAPTER THREE

Isabel knew straight away. She didn't need a doctor to tell her. She was only a week overdue, but she knew. Ever since she had started her periods she had been as regular as clockwork. The 'curse' arrived on time every time, but not this month. She was pregnant and knew exactly when it had happened. Panic had gripped her at first, how would she tell her mother? Could she get rid of it? Could it be adopted? Her mind was in turmoil. Would her mother be so ashamed of her that she would throw her out and if she did, where on earth could she go?

She said nothing for the next few days but the strain must have shown in her eyes. The Friday night shift had finished and arriving home she flopped into a chair and picked up the local paper, lit a cigarette and said nothing, not even acknowledging her mother.

Her mother looked up from her knitting. Her sad eyes bore into the back of Isabel until she had to turn and face her.

"I know," was all her mother said.

Isabel's mouth opened and closed but no words were spoken. The tears rolled down her cheeks as she stood, her mother's arms around her, neither wanting to let go, the invisible umbilical chord that could never be broken locked the two together.

After a while her mother released her and sat her down at the table. The quiet, insular woman who after her husband's death had retreated into her shell, suddenly morphed into an organiser par excellence.

She had obviously been thinking about the situation and had formulated a plan of action.

Isabel's mother had a cousin who had married a farmer who lived near Moreton-in-Marsh. Although she had not seen her for a couple of years they had been close as children and had become friends as well as being related. She had written to her cousin explaining the situation and asking if it would be possible for Isabel to stay with her until after the baby was born and that Isabel would earn her keep by helping on the farm up until the actual confinement. Her cousin was only too pleased to help and said she could come and stay as soon as she wished.

The next part of the plan was to 'create' a story for the friends and neighbours in Coventry. Isabel was surprised at her mother and could only marvel at her ingenuity.

Her mother outlined her scheme. She would tell everyone that Isabel had met a captain in the Royal Engineers and fallen in love. He had swept her of her feet, proposed, obtained a special licence and they had married secretly before he had been posted abroad. Her new husband had made her promise to leave the ambulance service and move and move to the country to live with his parents. They were farmers in the Cotswolds; she would be safer there too. After the baby had been born she could come back to Coventry, a grieving widow having heard that her new husband had been killed in action.

Isabel had to admit that the story was plausible. Lots of people met and married not knowing how long they would have, but snatching at any brief happiness that blotted out the agony of the war.

The whole thing made sense and Isabel squeezed her mother tight, the relief at sharing her dark secret with someone who she had most feared telling, was like opening a door into a sunlit garden.

Her mother looked at her daughter. Isabel was the only thing left in her life and she was not going to lose her, but there was an unanswered question hanging in the air. Who was the father?

As if by sixth sense Isabel knew what her mother was thinking. It was the look in her eyes, they bore deep into her conscience.

"He is a corporal in the army... home on leave... 24hr pass... his name is Mick... that's all I know. Do you hate me?" Isabel was crying as the words gushed out.

"No darling, I'm your mother I could never hate you. We all make mistakes."

They stood in each other's embrace, mother and daughter as one, both crying, the bond between them that had been stretched by the death of Isabel's father, now strong again.

CHAPTER FOUR

She bent down to pick up the post that was lying on the mat from the morning's delivery. Just the usual stuff; bills, junk mail, begging letters from charities she had never even heard of and free offers for goods she didn't want. She sifted through the envelopes and was about to throw most of them in the bin when one letter caught her eye. It had a London postmark on it, intrigued she opened it.

'Dear Mrs Harris,
"My firm act on behalf of the estate of one, Thomas Samuel Heaney, who died recently in a tragic road accident. In his will he left a bequest of a gold locket to a Jayne Brown whose last known address was Coundon Coventry. In his papers he states that he was asked to pass it on to Jayne Brown by his best friend Mick Furford, who he believes was killed in action during the Second World War.

I have spent some time and I might add expense, in trying to trace the lady in question and you are my last hope. The detective agency I use informs me that your maiden name was Brown and I wondered if in fact you might be the person I am seeking.

I would be grateful if you could contact me to discuss the matter.

Yours sincerely

Gerald Proctor
Proctor and Ives Solicitors

Jayne read the letter twice. Who on earth was Thomas Heaney and why would he want to give her a locket?

She needed to speak to her mother.

Jayne looked at her watch and realised she had spent longer than she thought reading and re-reading the solicitor's letter. It was 8.30 and she was normally at school by now. Grabbing her keys from the hall table and scooping up her briefcase she quickly exited the house and jumped into her car.

The day was uneventful. It was late June and the school term was winding down, most of the exams had finished and the curriculum completed. She had allowed her pupils 'free' time, which really meant nothing! The bell finally rang to put both teacher and pupils out of their misery. Driving home her mind went back to the letter she received that morning. She was puzzled, who on earth was Thomas Heaney? Her mother had never really talked about her natural father, other than to say he was in the army and was reported 'missing presumed killed in action' in Germany, and Jayne, having never known him, had not pursued the matter, but now she was curious, was Thomas Heaney him?

Her car turned into the drive and having locked the doors she went into her house. Walking straight through into the kitchen and stopping only to switch the electric kettle on, she picked up the letter and read it again.

The whistle of the boiling kettle broke into her thoughts and, almost on autopilot, she poured herself a cup of tea and took it into the living room.

She wanted to phone her mother straight away and confront her, to ask her who Heaney was, to ask questions that had for so long been left unasked. She looked at her watch; there was no point in ringing now as she knew her mother would be out visiting Grace, an old school friend who she had kept in touch with and now met at least once a week. She was tempted to ring the solicitors, but stopped herself as there was no point until she had discussed the letter with her mother.

Her friends had often asked her why she had not wanted to find out more about her father. What had happened to him? Had he survived the war? Why, if he had, did he not try and find her?

Each time these questions came up in conversation she would change the subject and now they stopped asking; but the letter had awakened a hidden curiosity that she had unconsciously suppressed until recently when she had, in her quiet moments, thought about him. Now she was intrigued and in her mind she imagined different scenarios as to what had happened to her father and why he had abandoned her.

Thank God term was winding down. Jayne had to admit to herself that the letter from the solicitors had fuelled her curiosity and she could not concentrate wholly on anything else. She thought it strange that for all these years she had either not bothered, or had suppressed any interest in her father and now this one letter had fuelled her imagination.

She had tried a couple of times to phone her mother, but each time only got the answerphone. She had left her name and said she would call back.

Saturday morning arrived and Jayne rang early, making sure she got her mother before she decided to go out to the shops. Jayne was nervous and wondered how her mother would react, after all it was a long time ago and they had never really discussed the matter, other than being told that her father had died.

The phone seemed to ring for ever, and she was about to give up and replace the receiver, when her mother answered. She had been in the shower and had not heard the phone at first. Jayne quickly told her about the letter from the solicitors and read it to her in full. When she had finished she asked point blank.

"Was Thomas Heaney my father?"

Her mother suppressed a laugh.

"Your father's name was Mick. I don't know of a Thomas Heaney, although he did have a friend called Tommy."

Jayne was even more confused. She said she would contact the solicitors on Monday and let her mother know what happened. They spoke for a further half an hour about nothing in particular, the normal chat that was now a Saturday ritual.

Nigel came down for his breakfast and asked if that was 'Gran' on the phone? He had been strangely quiet for the last few days and Jayne had not seen a lot of him, in fact had not even had a chance to tell him about the letter.

She went through to the kitchen and made some toast and a fresh pot of tea, setting them down on the table; she pulled up a chair beside him and spread the letter out in front of him.

Nigel was intrigued, and asked his mother what she was going to do?

It would be interesting to know about his grandfather. He had once brought the subject up with his grandmother and he remembered she had looked at him and said that he had his grandfather's eyes. He was sure he had seen a tear appear in her eyes. He had pressed her to talk about him, but she had changed the subject and no amount of pressure would change her mind. Now, with the letter his mother had received, maybe some light would be thrown on the mystery.

Jayne told him she would contact Mr Proctor on Monday, and brushed aside all of Nigel's theories on what the outcome might be. There was no point in speculating; hopefully her meeting with the solicitor would provide the answers to their questions.

Jayne had made up her mind she would call in on her mother the next day and find out more about 'Mick'!

CHAPTER FIVE

Isabel kept to the story that her mother had suggested. On the following Monday she spoke to her supervisor at the ambulance station and told him that she was sorry but she would be leaving as she was getting married. Her future husband had insisted that it would be safer to live at his parents' house in the country. Her boss was disappointed as she had been one of his most reliable drivers, never missing a shift since she had joined. However, he graciously wished her well and congratulated her on her 'whirlwind romance'.

Grace was next on her list. She could not lie to Grace; they had been close friends through school and had always confided in each other.

Grace gasped when Isabel told her she was pregnant and explained that her mother had devised a scheme to cover the confinement. Who would have thought that Mrs Brown would have the ingenuity to suggest such a thing?

Isabel swore her friend to secrecy and said she would write to her from the farm, in fact she was sure her cousin would not mind if she visited.

Needless to say, Grace wanted to know all the details and especially who the father was. When Isabel reminded her of the night that they met the two soldiers, Mick and Tommy, Grace giggled. Strangely, the two girls had never discussed that evening before.

"I guess I was the lucky one then. It could easily have been me sneaking off to the country." Grace's admission made Isabel smile. The bond between the two friends seemed even stronger now.

She left Grace and walked the short distance back to her mother's house. Mrs Brown had a kettle already boiling, as if she had sensed her daughter's arrival. She poured two cups of tea and set them down on the table. Isabel marvelled at the change in her mother since she had told her about the baby. It was as if a new life force had entered her, given her a reason to exist!

"Are you going to find the father and tell him?" Isabel had not even thought about the father. "I think you should."

Isabel did not sleep well that night, her mind going over the question her mother had posed. She realised that she did not know anything about Mick, other than he was in the army. Should she try and find him? Would he even accept responsibility? After all, it had been a one night stand, no commitment, just satisfying a need, they both had known that. She tossed and turned wondering, one minute deciding he had the right to know, the next thinking he would walk away and deny everything. So why tell him? Eventually she fell asleep, the problem still unresolved.

The next morning was bright and sunny. As she drew her curtains and surveyed the fresh green of the trees with the sunlight playing on the morning dew, she reached a decision.

She would wait until the baby had been born and then find Mick and tell him. She had reasoned that she might have a miscarriage, lots of first time pregnancies did not go to full term, and, if that happened, what was the point in telling him.

Her mother felt he should know straightaway, but Isabel was adamant and so did not labour the point

Whilst Isabel had been worrying about informing Mick, even finding him, her mother had been busily 'setting the scene' with the neighbours. She had told them and in fact anybody who was remotely interested, including old Mrs Haynes in the paper shop, about the good news that Isabel was getting married to a captain no less. Telling Mrs Haynes was a masterstroke because that guaranteed more people knowing than an advert in the *Coventry Evening Telegraph*!

One or two of her friends expressed a little 'surprise' at the suddenness of it all, but Mrs Brown soon convinced them that with the war, youngsters felt they had no time to lose and the bridegroom was on standby to be sent abroad at any moment.

The weekend was spent packing clothes for her stay at her cousin's. Isabel had checked the trains and found that there was a train from Leamington Spa on Monday morning. That would take her to Evesham and her cousin's husband would collect her to take her to the farm. She would have to get a bus from Coventry to Leamington Spa, but this was no problem as there was a regular service between the two. Her mother wanted to go with her, but Isabel persuaded her that there was no point and she finally conceded defeat.

Isabel had been sensible and packed clothes that would be ideal for working and every day use, she would not be needing fancy dresses or high heeled shoes for some time! Fortunately she was proficient with a needle and thread and had decided to make her own alterations as she filled out during the oncoming months.

Monday soon came and her mother insisted on paying for a taxi and accompanying her daughter to the bus station.

When the bus arrived her mother hugged her and made her promise to write letting her know how things were. A tear ran down her cheek as she kissed her mother and thanked her for everything. It was a wrench leaving but she knew that it was her mother's plan and a good one at that; after all, once the baby had arrived she would be home straight away.

Bob and Shirley were at the station waiting for her. Both were in their early fifties and had the typical ruddy complexions that came from working outdoors in all weathers. Bob had inherited the farm from his father and had worked on the land all his life. Shirley was originally from Coventry, but her parents had moved to Moreton-in-Marsh when her father, a bank manager, had been transferred to the local branch. They had settled on the slower moving life away from the city and her father had refused any further moves, even though it had meant missing out on promotion. Bob and Shirley had fallen in love in their teens but had waited until he was twenty-one before they wed.

Shirley soon learnt about farming and being a farmer's wife.

Because his farm was mostly arable and home grown food was desperately needed, he was exempt from serving in the forces, farming having been designated a 'reserve occupation' for the duration of the war.

Shirley held out her arms to greet her cousin's daughter. She was looking forward to having her stay with them. Their house had felt empty for many years, their only son having died from tuberculosis when he was only eleven years old.

"Isabel, gosh how you have grown it must be ten years since I last saw you." She smiled as she pulled Isabel to her and squeezed hard, taking her breath away. "Sorry, this is Bob, my husband." She turned and pointed to Bob.

Bob moved forward and shook her hand; he was not a demonstrative man.

"It's good to see you both and I really appreciate you taking me in like this," her voice faltered slightly.

She was embarrassed and Shirley quickly picked up on the situation.

"Come on, let's get back to the farm, have a cup of tea and get you settled in. We can then talk about how you can earn your keep."

She smiled, a lovely warm smile that made everyone instantly trust her and feel somehow protected. Bob was the quiet reliable type and Isabel could see how they complemented each other. This was definitely a happy home and any forebodings Isabel had were quickly dispelled.

Bob picked up her case and carried it to the truck that was parked outside the station. They all squeezed onto the bench seat in the cab and Bob started the engine. The old crash box crunched as he selected first gear and they pulled away. The farm was only ten miles from the station and they were soon there. Isabel looked at the cottage. It was small but very pretty with climbing roses growing either side of the door. It was just as she had pictured it in her mind.

Shirley ushered her into the house and straight up the stairs to the room which would be her sanctuary for the next eight to nine months. Bob followed them with her case and having deposited it on the bed, disappeared downstairs. There were only two bedrooms and the bathroom on the first floor.

Isabel followed Shirley down to the kitchen, which was the hub of the house. It was the biggest room, with a range on one side and a table at the other. A large sink with draining board sat below the window overlooking the courtyard. The living room was seldom used except by Bob for keeping all his farm records and papers. The radio was on a shelf just to the right of the sink. The radio was all important as it kept them in touch with the outside world and how the war was going. Since Dunkirk there were always rumours of when Britain would go back to liberate Europe but, as the days passed, it was obvious that the country would need to build its resources if it was not to suffer the same fate as the British Expeditionary Force.

Shirley filled the kettle and put it on top of the range and, while waiting for it to boil, reached into the cupboard for two mugs, Bob having gone out into the fields to continue the never-ending work of the farm.

With the steaming mug of rich brown tea and a large slice of home made currant cake, Isabel relaxed into her new surroundings.

"I warn you we get up at six every morning; in fact many mornings Bob is up at five." Shirley flashed her smile again. "Your job will be to feed the chickens and pigs and clean them out while I milk the cows. We only have a few cows mainly for milk for our own use. After that we can stop for breakfast. Bob makes sure that he comes in for breakfast; he thinks it's the most important meal of the day. After breakfast I usually do the baking and preparing the vegetables for the evening meal. Sandwiches for lunch and it will be your job to take them out to Bob and the lads, wherever they are working. It's not a huge farm so you will soon find your way around the fields. In the afternoon I sometimes go to market, or help the vicar at the church, or go to a WI meeting and... well, there is always something happening." She stopped talking to let what she had said sink in.

Strangely Isabel was not fazed by all she had heard; in fact she was quite looking forward to it. She had never been afraid of hard work and it would be a relief to get away from all the death and destruction that she had been used to.

"Shirley, honestly I am looking forward to it. If you had seen some of the sights I have seen over the past months then you'd know what I mean."

"Great, well you go and unpack and then I'll give you a quick tour so that you will be able to get your bearings for tomorrow."

That night Isabel lay on her bed content that she was in good hands. Her only apprehension was the thought of actually having the baby and what would happen after that.

CHAPTER SIX

Jayne sat reading a magazine, the chatter of the receptionist putting calls through to the different offices, a dull drone in the background. Her appointment with Mr Proctor was for 11 o'clock and she had made sure that, if anything, she was a little early, so she was getting slightly irritated by being kept waiting fifteen minutes already! Why do solicitors and doctors bother making appointments when they never keep to the times arranged? The thought passed through her mind as she flipped through the pages of the *Country Life* magazine, which was three months out of date anyway.

The clock slowly moved its hands round and now showed 11.30. Maybe she would just walk out if he hadn't the manners to keep to the time agreed. Before she could make her mind up the receptionist leaned across her desk to say that Mr Proctor would see her now.

Jayne stood up, smoothing her skirt down as she did so, and followed the girl through the door and down the corridor. Proctor's office was the third door along on the left and the girl knocked and walked in.

"Mrs Harris," she announced, then turned and left.

"Mrs Harris, sorry to keep you." Mr Proctor was a short man with a rounded face that sported a large walrus moustache. He looked less like a solicitor than she could have imagined. He beckoned her to take a seat and opened a file on his desk.

"Thank you for coming all this way. It will be a relief to finally put this matter to bed." His eyes never left the file as he spoke. "As I explained in my letter, my client's will specifically asked that the locket be passed onto Jayne Brown, who it appears was the daughter of his friend, Mick Furford. Mr Furford had asked him to look after it when he was posted to the South Coast as part of the invasion force in the war. My client could not join the invasion as he had sadly lost his leg in an accident and was transferred to a desk job. Anyway, to continue, I understand from talking to my client's son, that the two friends lost contact and he believed that Mr Furford was killed in action. For many years my client forgot about the locket and it was only in the last years of his life, after he had moved to a new house, that the locket came to light again. I understand he felt guilty that he had let his friend down, hence the specific clause asking that we find his friend's daughter." Mr Proctor took a deep breath as he finally looked up from his papers.

"I take it you have brought some proof of your identity?" he asked.

"Yes. I have my birth certificate, but there is no name of my father on it. My mother was not married when I was born; she told me that my father was in the Army and believed he had been killed whilst fighting in Germany. I was not aware that he even knew I existed."

Jayne passed the certificate across the desk. The solicitor examined it, appeared satisfied then picked up the phone and asked his secretary to come in and take a copy for his records. He replaced the receiver then stood up, crossed the room to where a large old-fashioned safe stood next to a bookcase laden with law books. Opening the safe he reached inside and withdrew a small narrow box about eight inches long. He returned to his chair and placing the box on the desk, opened it to reveal a gold chain with a square shaped locket on it. He passed the locket to Jayne.

Jayne took the chain and opened the locket to reveal a portrait of a beautiful woman probably in her twenties. The picture was faded and obviously taken many years ago. Jayne was puzzled because the picture was definitely not of her mother, so who could it be?

Mr Proctor coughed politely, to get Jayne's attention.

"If you could just sign this letter, which states that you have taken possession of the locket, then I have fulfilled my obligations."

Jayne signed, without really reading what she was signing for, her mind was far from the offices of Proctor and Ives. She was wondering who the woman in the portrait was and why the locket was important. It was gold and therefore worth something, but not thousands of pounds. No, there was something more, but what, she had no idea.

On returning home she opened the door and made straight for the phone. She had promised her mother that she would let her know what had happened at the solicitors, more importantly she had some questions to ask her mother!

The phone seemed to ring for ever before her mother answered.

"Mum?"

"Yes."

"I've just got back from the solicitors. I have the locket, inside there is a picture of a woman." She paused to see if there would be a reaction to this, but her mother said nothing. "It appears that this Thomas Heaney was asked to pass the locket to me by his friend, Mick Furford."

The mention of the name Mick Furford brought an intake of breath from her mother which Jayne quickly picked up on.

"Was Mick Furford my father?"

"Yes."

"Did you tell him about me? What happened to him?" There were so many questions she wanted to ask but didn't know where to start.

"I tried to tell him. I went to his camp looking for him. I only knew his first name and there were a few Micks in the regiment." She gave a short laugh at the memory. "However, the officer I spoke to was very helpful. When I gave him a brief description and told him that he had a best friend called Tommy, he spoke to his sergeant who knew Mick and Tommy and said it had to be Mick Furford. I told the lieutenant about you and left my details, asking him to get Mick to contact me if he wanted to see you."

"So did he contact you?"

"No. I waited and waited but assumed that he didn't want to accept responsibility. You've got to understand things were different then. The war affected people differently, life was cheap and you lived for the day. In a strange way I understood and didn't blame him. The months went by and nothing happened. When the allies invaded France, thousands died and I got it into my mind that he had been killed in action. I had no proof but I suppose it's what I wanted to believe. I could not accept that he had just deserted us."

Jayne listened to her mother in silence. How could she have made love to a man whose name she didn't even know? She realised how little she really knew about her mother.

"Well, he must have thought of us somehow because he entrusted his friend with this locket and it was obviously of some value, either monetarily or sentimentally." Jayne was still puzzled by the photograph, but couldn't think how it could be significant.

"Do you want me to come over?" her mother asked.

"No... no... I'll show you the locket when I see you next. It's probably not worth all that much anyway."

The line went dead and Jayne went into the kitchen to make a cup of tea. She had a locket which her father had obviously felt was important enough for him to entrust to his friend to ensure she got it, but after all these years did it matter? Her father had never been a part of her life and now all of a sudden she could not get him out her mind. The locket told her nothing. She took it out of its box and examined it, looking on the back for any inscription, but there was nothing. She opened the locket and on an impulse removed the picture from its frame, turning it over she saw some writing in tiny neat script.

'To my darling Florence, my fondest love George D.'

Jayne was even more puzzled now and no nearer finding out what had happened to her father.

She was still sitting drinking her tea, the locket lying on the table, when Nigel came in. He kissed his mother and seeing the locket asked, "Is that what all the fuss is about?"

Jayne smiled, he was right. Perhaps she was making a mountain out of a very little molehill. She relayed the events of the day: the trip to the solicitors and her phone conversation with her mother.

"Bit of a lass, our Gran!" he said with a grin from ear to ear.

Jayne reproached him, defending her mother by explaining that in the war it was different, exactly the same explanation that her mother had given her.

CHAPTER SEVEN

Isabel had quickly got used to the routine of the farm. The biggest difference from her city life was that every day was much the same, there were no weekends off. The animals needed feeding and cleaning no matter what the day was and that included Christmas. She didn't mind because she felt safe and away from the misery of the bombing. That night in November had been the worst but, although it was less intense, there were still raids on the factories and the City was on constant alert. She missed her mother and worried about her so wrote every week, although, as the weeks went by, it was hard to find something different to tell her. The work was physically tiring but satisfying and, now that spring was well under way, the temperature was beginning to rise and the mornings felt fresh. In this particular corner of England you could momentarily forget about the war and all the pain and suffering.

Because Bob grew most of the vegetables they needed, there was no shortage of fresh food or need for ration books. Consequently, Isabel was in the best of health and felt confident that the baby that was growing large inside her would be well nourished when it arrived. She was now nearly seven months pregnant and the 'bump' was well pronounced. Shirley had reduced her work load to take into account her lack of mobility, but Isabel wanted to pull her weight, after all she was grateful that they had taken her in to their home and made her one of the family.

Shirley had never asked her about the baby's father and Isabel had not brought the subject up. It had become an unwritten rule that it would not be discussed. There was no need to go into any details. Isabel was sure that her mother had discussed the situation with her cousin when she first asked if Isabel could stay with her.

Although they never talked about it, nevertheless, Isabel often thought about Mick. She was not in love with him, how could she be, they had only met once, but they had a bond. It was their child that was growing inside her and she felt that Mick had the right to know that. She resolved to find him and tell him about the baby once it had been born. Whether he would want to have anything to do with her once he knew, she didn't know, but he definitely did have the right.

Having made up her mind on the course of action she would take once back in Coventry, she felt as though a weight had been lifted from her shoulders. After writing to her mother and telling her what she planned to do, she was pleased that her mother had replied, fully supporting her decision.

The next two months flew by, the days blurring into one as her delivery date approached.

Shirley was in the cowshed, having just finished the milking, when she heard the scream. In her rush she nearly knocked over the pail of fresh milk, but just managed to save it as she ran to the door. Another wail, louder than the first, was coming from the farmhouse kitchen. Breathless, she threw open the door to see Isabel bent almost double over the sink, tears streaming down her cheeks. A wet pool slowly spreading across the kitchen floor told Shirley that there would be no time to get Isabel to the bed that had been booked at the cottage hospital.

Shirley was not fazed by the scene that met her. Over the years she had helped deliver calves and pigs so a baby couldn't be that different. She grabbed some towels and spread them over the couch in the living room then went back for Isabel. They managed to shuffle into the room and Isabel lay back on the couch her cries more muted now, but more often. Shirley took the opportunity to phone the midwife, who briefly gave some instructions on what to do and promised to be with them in fifteen minutes. Shirley smiled to herself, in fifteen minutes it would be all over, of that she was sure.

When the midwife finally arrived, the fifteen minutes being nearly an hour, Isabel was sitting cradling her newborn baby girl in her arms. Shirley was in the kitchen boiling a kettle having anticipated that the midwife would want a cup of tea before anything else.

Siobhan Maloney, the district midwife, was fulsome in her praise of Shirley who blushed when she was told what a magnificent job she had done and she should consider taking up midwifery.

"I have my hands full with the farm and I'm sure Bob wouldn't be too pleased if I took up your idea."

Siobhan washed the baby and wrapped her in the shawl that Isabel's mother had given to her before she went away. It had been the one she had when Isabel was born.

"A nice easy routine birth, I wish they were all like that," she said. "Have you chosen a name yet?"

In truth, Isabel had not even thought of a name for a boy or a girl and now wondered whether she should wait until she had spoken to Mick about her. She wished her mother was here to ask her opinion.

Before Siobhan left she and Shirley helped Isabel upstairs and into bed. The baby was fast asleep in her cot next to Isabel's bed and as soon as the two women had left the room the sound of heavy breathing indicated she too had joined her daughter.

Isabel woke next morning to be greeted by the sound of crying from the tiny bundle next to her. This is something I am going to have to get used to, she thought, but it was a pleasant thought and she couldn't wait to pick the child from its cot and stare at the tiny features. Tears of happiness and relief trickled down her cheeks, right now there was no war, no killing and destruction, only this beautiful new life. She had made a decision. She had been reading *Emma* by Jane Austin. She would call the baby Jane, but spelt Jayne, for no other reason than to be different. Her daughter was different... she was special.

Isabel wanted desperately to tell her mother of the arrival of Jayne, but as there was no phone at her mother's house she could not call direct. A telegram was the logical answer, although a telegram usually filled the recipient with fear as it often brought news of death. Since the death of her father, her mother had an irrational fear of telegrams. It was Shirley who solved the problem, suggesting that Isabel should phone Mrs Haynes who owned the newsagents and ask her to pass the news on to her mother.

Isabel liked the idea at first but did not want anybody else to know the news before her mother, if old blabber-mouth Haynes knew then the whole street would know in no time.

Isabel thought for a moment then smiled.

"What do you think about this?" she asked Shirley. "I'll ask her to tell Mum 'the package arrived safe and sound tied in pink ribbon'."

"Brilliant!" Shirley exclaimed.

"I'll send her a letter with all the details but at least she will know we're all right."

The next few days seemed to drag as all Isabel could do was wash and feed the baby then sit around the house whilst she slept. She did not feel strong enough to do any physical work and felt a fraud as she was not pulling her weight. Shirley and Bob had no truck with such thoughts and doted on the baby as if it was their own grandchild. Isabel wanted to get back to Coventry but knew she must keep the pretence up until she could return as the grieving widow.

The baby had been born on the 28th of July and it was now the second week of August. Shirley had noticed her frustration and realised that Isabel had to leave or she would get too distressed and then the baby might suffer. Much as part of her wanted Isabel to stay longer she knew she would have to go.

That morning after she had finished the milking and seeing to the pigs, she came into the kitchen where Isabel was sitting reading the paper.

"I'll help you pack your bags and then Bob can run us to the station, there's a train to Leamington Spa at twelve o'clock. Bob wants you to have this money so that you can get a taxi from the station to your mum's without having to mess about with buses.

Isabel's eyes lit up at the thought of going home, but part of her was sad. Shirley and Bob had been like second parents to her and had made her feel part of the family. She felt slightly ashamed that she should be happy at leaving them. It was typical of Bob that he had offered to pay for a taxi and she knew he would be offended if she refused to accept his generosity.

"I don't know what to say... you've been so kind to me... I don't know what I would have done without you both." Her voice choked as the tears welled up in her eyes.

Shirley came round the table and hugged her. She was crying now. They stayed locked together for the moment, a bond forged between two women that usually only happens between mother and daughter. They wiped their eyes and smiled at each other. Nothing needed to be said, they both knew that there would always be a special knot that now tied them.

Bob parked the truck in the car park and lifted the case from the back while Shirley went to the ticket office to collect Isabel's ticket and two platform tickets for her and Bob. They did not have long to wait before the clouds of smoke heralded the arrival of the train. Bob opened the carriage door and, stepping inside, lifted the case onto the luggage rack. Isabel was having one last hug with Shirley. Bob kissed her on the cheek and wished her good luck, making her promise to visit them so they could see little Jayne growing up. Isabel felt a tear roll down her cheek as she waved goodbye. The shrill whistle of the guard heralding a new chapter in her life as the train slowly pulled away from the station.

CHAPTER EIGHT

Jayne was flustered and that was not like her. Ever since getting the locket she had not been able to concentrate, constantly going over in her mind the significance of it. Fortunately, school term had finished but she had promised to organise a family night out for Nigel's eighteenth birthday. Now it was only two days away and she hadn't even booked the restaurant. Luckily the day fell on a Wednesday and she felt sure the restaurant would not be full. To make matters worse, Ron had phoned and said he would not be able to make his son's party, as his current girlfriend had booked a week's holiday in Spain.

"I bet the bitch did that on purpose," she said under her breath.

At least James would be home from university and Nigel had said he would be bringing Clare. Jayne had not met Clare but felt sure Nigel had been seeing her for some time. It was odd that he had not brought her home before as he had done with all his past girlfriends, of which there had been many. Maybe this one was different.

Jayne had asked Nigel if he had any special restaurant that he would like to go to, but all she got back was "you choose".

It was at times like these that she realised that husbands do have their uses. She laughed to herself; they sometimes have other uses as well she thought.

She reached for the telephone directory and set about the task of finding a nice restaurant that would be special, but not break the bank at the same time. It was a task that was to prove more difficult than first imagined and it was two hours before she finally put the phone down, having booked a table at 'Chez Thomas'.

"I just hope he likes it," she said out loud.

James had arrived home on the afternoon of his brother's birthday, having spent a few days staying with friends following the end of term. The brothers had spent most of the afternoon catching up with each other's news and Jayne had not really had chance to talk to James, but was content in the knowledge that he would be with her for the next eight weeks, so she would have plenty of time to talk to him. Anyway, it was Nigel's day and she was happy that the two were so close; it had not always been that way.

The restaurant had been booked for seven thirty and she had ordered a taxi to collect them at seven. It was a surprise, therefore, when, at five, Nigel came downstairs already changed and said that he was going to collect Clare and would meet them at the restaurant.

"But I thought she was coming here and we would all go together," Isabel protested.

"No Mum, I'll see you there."

There was no argument: he had decided.

James smiled at his mother.

"What's the problem Mum? If that's what he wants, it's his birthday."

"Yes I suppose you're right," she replied rather reluctantly.

"Anyway, if we've got an hour to spare before we get ready, are you going to tell me about this locket? Nigel has filled me in with some of the details, especially the bit about gran being a bit of a devil." He laughed, and as he knew she would, his mother leapt in to defend his grandmother's honour.

"You don't understand there was a war on, things were different."

"That's exactly what Nigel said you would say." He laughed again.

"Don't tease."

She moved across the room to the bureau and pulled down the top, reached inside, withdrew the box that held the locket and handed it to James, who opened the box to examine it.

"Very pretty," he said as he opened the catch on the front to reveal the picture. Turning the locket over he noticed the back was black with dirt. Reaching into his pocket, he pulled out his handkerchief and, spitting on it, used it to rub the dirt away.

"There's something on the back."

Isabel leaned over to get a better look but could see nothing.

"Let me get the magnifying glass from the bureau."

She came back with the glass and by now James had cleaned even more of the dirt off to reveal the shape of what looked like a shield. He held the glass close to the locket. It was indeed a shield with chevrons on it and what appeared to be two lions either side. Under the shield was a scroll, but it was not clear what had been written on it.

"I would guess it's some kind of coat of arms. I'll take a picture of it, go to the library and see if I can find out the family it belongs to, if you like. It might give you some clue to who your dad is."

Jayne was puzzled. Her mother had told her that her father's name was Mick Furford and he had been just a corporal in the army, certainly not the sort of person to have a family crest. Her thoughts were broken by the clock chiming six.

"Come on, we had better get ready or we'll be late for your brother."

James put the locket back in its box and returned it to the bureau, his mother having already gone upstairs to change.

Jayne was ready just in time. She reached the bottom of the stairs as the taxi drew up outside. James checked that everywhere was locked up and, making sure that he had his front door key, followed her into the taxi.

Jayne was relieved that when they arrived at the restaurant Nigel was not already there. She wanted to have a bottle of champagne opened ready to greet him. She was looking forward to meeting Clare, who was obviously special or he would not have been hiding her all this time.

When Nigel walked into the room and was shown to the table where his mother and brother were already seated, there was a sharp intake of breath from Jayne. Clare was indeed different from all his past girlfriends...

...she was black!

CHAPTER NINE

Isabel was glad to be home. Although Shirley and Bob had been good to her, she had been surprised how much she had missed her mother. Her mother almost fell over the front door mat in her rush to greet her daughter and new granddaughter.

"Oh... she's beautiful... let me hold her."

Isabel smiled as she passed the bundle to her mother, "I am calling her Jayne," she said.

Her mother had not heard, she was totally absorbed by the child.

"Shall we go inside? The neighbours will be wondering why we are standing outside, they'll think you don't want me back." Isabel was grinning as she spoke and it had the desired effect of bringing her mother out of her trance.

"Oh God I'm sorry. It's so good to see you. I've missed you so much and of course was worried, that is until I got your message that 'the parcel had arrived safely tied with pink ribbon'." They both laughed at their shared subterfuge.

Isabel eventually managed to extract the baby from her mother's arms and laid her in the cot that she noticed in the corner. It was so like her mother to have everything prepared.

They left the baby to sleep and went to the kitchen. Two cups of tea later, Mrs Brown had heard all about the farm, the birth and how wonderful Shirley and Bob had been.

"Mum, I want to keep in touch with them, without their kindness I don't know how I would have managed."

"We will, but first we have to get our story right. The whole street knows you are home and it won't be long before they come knocking on the door asking what has happened."

They went over the story that they had planned nine months ago. 'Within two weeks of the birth, Isabel had received a telegram informing her that her husband, Captain Charles Davenport, had been killed in action in Egypt. She had not seen her husband since shortly after they were married, as he had been posted abroad. Isabel was living with her parents-in-law just outside Moreton-in-Marsh. Of course, both of his parents were devastated and had said there was a home for Isabel and her new baby with them as long as she wanted, but Isabel hardly knew them and wanted to be back with her mother.'

"I think that sounds plausible, but you must remember to look depressed and sad for a few weeks. People will expect you to be mourning, especially as you were both 'so in love'." Her mother looked pleased with herself. "I think we will try it on old Mrs Haynes first. If she goes along with it then she will convince everyone else." She could not resist a little grin.

Mrs Haynes was horrified when she was told the news and offered any help she could to Isabel and the baby. Isabel could not help feeling a little guilty at her duplicity, but her guilt did not last long.

Within a couple of weeks of returning home Isabel and the baby were accepted within the neighbourhood and life returned to normal, that is the normality of an insane world riven with death and destruction.

Isabel was finding being at home all day, with nothing to do except feed and care for the baby, beginning to play on her nerves. Her mother was kind and helpful but in an interfering way that was annoying. She realised that having 'two' mothers was not good for little Jayne and not good for her either.

That evening she had cleared away the dishes, Jayne was already fast asleep, and sat down next to her mother who was well into her latest knitting project.

"Mum... I was wondering if I could go back to work... perhaps part-time at first..." She didn't finish the sentence.

"What about the baby? Have you thought about that?" Her mother had put down her knitting and was looking at her. Her brow furrowed, her mouth just a thin line.

"Well... I had hoped you would look after her for the hours I worked..." Her words trailed away, hoping her mother would pick up on the suggestion. "I would like to go back to driving for the ambulance service." She knew her mother approved of the work the service did and hoped that would be enough to swing it.

"I think the baby is a little young, but if you only work a half a day I suppose I can't really say no. Only half a day mind you, at least until she is six months old."

"Mum, you're wonderful. I promise only half a day and I'll make up Jayne's bottles before I leave. With her sleeping most of the morning you'll hardly know she's there."

"Now I want you to do something for me. You said you would contact Jayne's father and tell him about the baby. I think you should do that without any further delay."

She knew her mother was right, having made her own mind up to try to find him. However, for some reason she had kept putting it off. Now she would have to make the effort or she would not be going back to work.

"I want you to speak to him before you contact the service to say you want to come back. I know you, if you don't make contact you will let it drift and before you know it Jayne will be going to school!"

Isabel was a little miffed at her mother's remark but said nothing. In her heart she knew she was right.

The following Saturday, with Grace in tow to give her some much needed Dutch courage, she set out for Pool Meadow Bus Station to catch the bus that would take them to Bramcote Barracks, not far from Nuneaton town. Grace had been the one who had remembered one of the boys mentioning that they were stationed at Bramcote and, although it was the best part of a year since the night of the dance, there was still a chance that they hadn't been posted to another barracks.

Isabel had wondered exactly what to say, after all, she only knew his name was Mick, they had not got round to exchanging surnames or life histories!

The bus dropped them at the end of Marston Lane. The driver had told them that the main gates were about half a mile along the lane, just after the road curved round to the right.

As they approached the gates a sentry came out of the gate hut and asked if he could help them.

"Would it be possible to see your commanding officer? I am trying to trace a soldier." Isabel tried to control her nervousness and hoped the sentry did not pick up on it. She had decided to ask for the commanding officer in the hope that it would sound important enough for someone to speak to her.

"Do you have this soldier's name?" the sentry demanded.

"I only have his first name I'm afraid, but it is very important."

"I'll ring the office and see if anyone will see you," he said almost dismissively.

After a wait of about five minutes he came out of his hut.

"You're in luck, the C.O.'s out but Lieutenant Jacobs will see you. He's sending someone down to escort you to his office."

They were left standing outside the gates, the sentry having returned to his hut. Fortunately the weather was warm and dry, but Isabel suspected that even if it had been pouring with rain they would still be standing in exactly the same spot.

A further twenty minutes elapsed before a young soldier, who looked as if he had only just left school, walked up to the sentry's hut and after a brief word, the barrier that acted as the gate was lifted, and they were beckoned through.

They passed rows of huts, which were obviously the living quarters of the soldiers, round a corner where a large concrete building, painted in camouflage colours faced them. Four steps led up to the double doors.

The soldier knocked the door and waited until he heard what sounded like a bark, which was the signal for them to enter. They followed him inside, where a sergeant sat behind a desk with a large typewriter dominating most of its surface.

The sergeant pointed to two chairs and indicated that they should sit down. He did not speak and hardly looked up whist they followed his instructions. Another wait, the only noise the rattle of the typewriter as he continued with his paperwork. The two women looked at each other neither daring to break the silence for fear of some reprimand. Eventually the sergeant stood up and, shuffling a number of papers together, disappeared through a door to his right. With only a perfunctory knock he entered without waiting for any acknowledgement. He reappeared and looking at the women, crooked his little finger gesturing them to come into the inner office.

Behind the desk a young man in his early twenties rose to greet them.

"Lieutenant Jacobs," he said by way of introduction. "How can I help you?"

"I'm Isabel Brown and this is my friend Grace Furnish. I'm looking for a soldier but I only know his first name... Mick." Isabel realised how foolish she must sound.

"We have a number of Micks, Mikes and Michaels in the regiment, do you have anything else to go on?" Lt. Jacobs had a kindly smile and sounded as though he genuinely wanted to help. "Can you tell me why exactly you need to contact him?"

The two women looked at each other. Isabel knew she would have to tell him if they were to stand any chance of finding Mick.

"I've recently had a baby girl and Mick is the father," she blurted out.

The officer raised his eyebrows but said nothing. The silence was deafening.

"He had a close friend called Tommy if that's any help." Grace broke the silence.

"Let me ask my sergeant, there's not much goes on round here that he doesn't know about." He walked around the desk to the door connecting to the outer office, pulling it open he called to the man who was bent over his desk to come in. "Sergeant, do you know of a couple of squaddies who knock around together called Mick and Tommy, supposedly close friends?"

"Yes, sir, Corporal Mick Furford and Private Thomas Heany, they're almost joined at the hip.

"Right, then get Corporal Furford in here straight away, this young lady needs to speak to him."

"Sorry, sir, that won't be possible. They're both up north on manoeuvres."

"Oh yes, sorry, I should have realised. Thank you sergeant, that will be all."

Once the sergeant had left the room the lieutenant turned to Isabel.

"Miss Brown, if you would like to leave your details with me, I will ensure Corporal Furford is informed of your visit and ask him to contact you."

"Thank you, would you also tell him the baby's name is Jayne." She stood up and wrote her name and address on the piece of paper that was pushed towards her.

The officer placed the paper in his in-tray and pressed a buzzer on his desk to summon the sergeant, the meeting was over.

The gate dropped shut behind them and they were again in the lane walking to the main road to await the next bus back to Coventry. Nothing was said for a while until Grace voiced the thought that both had been dwelling on: "Would Mick in fact make contact?"

CHAPTER TEN

Mick and Tommy threw their kit bags in a heap at the bottom of their bunks. Like their comrades they were exhausted. Coming back to camp after two weeks on the Yorkshire moors was like returning to a five star hotel. At least the camp had hot water for washing, toilets and passably good food, though no one would admit that to Cookie.

Mick lit two cigarettes and passed one to Tommy, then stretched out on his bunk inhaling the smoke slowly. His eyes closed, not in sleep but relaxation. His reverie did not last long. Sergeant Collins burst into the room barking his name.

"Furford... Lieutenant Jacobs wants you in his office at the double... come on man shift your arse... you've just had a fortnight's holiday."

Mick swung his legs over the side of the bunk.

"What's this all about, Sarge?"

"You'll find out if you get moving over to the office, won't you?" Collins glared at him.

Mick stubbed his cigarette out, picked up his beret put it on and had a quick look in the mirror to check that his tunic was buttoned up correctly, before following the sergeant to the office.

He stood to attention facing the lieutenant, who was busy signing forms, waiting for him to speak.

"At ease, Corporal." The officer put his pen down and looked up. "I had a visit from a young lady last week by the name of Isabel Brown. Does the name ring any bells?"

Mick racked his brains, trying to remember if he had heard the name before, but nothing came to mind.

"Should I know this lady, sir?"

"Well she claims to know you... intimately. She claims you are the father of her baby."

Mick let out a gasp of surprise. Who on earth could this person be? He had had lots of dates and slept with some of them, but was sure that he had been careful.

"Would it help if I showed you her address?" He passed a sheet of paper across the desk and Mick picked it up.

'2, Donnington Road, Coundon, Coventry.'

He read it three times before a sudden realisation dawned on him... Isabel... Coundon. Oh God! now I remember. His mind went back to the night of the dance, almost a year ago. It had been passionate, beautiful, but over all too soon and no he had not been careful that night!

"Sir, yes I do know the lady. What does she want me to do?"

"Nothing if you don't want to. She left these contact details and to tell you that you had a daughter whose name I believe is Jayne, if you want to see her and the baby then to get in touch with her. You have all the details on that piece of paper."

Mick saluted, turned and left the office his mind in a whirl.

Tommy was keen to find out why his friend had been summoned to Jacobs' office in such a hurry and feared it might be some bad news about his family. Mick walked into the hut still in a daze.

"Christ Mick, you're as white as a ghost, is it bad news?"

"I'm not sure really," he replied.

"What on earth do you mean? Has someone died?"

"Quite the reverse actually."

Tommy was confused; his friend was not making any sense and seemed to be on another planet.

"Are you going to tell me what happened, or do I have to go and ask Jacobs myself?"

"I'm a father," he blurted out.

"A bloody what?" Tommy asked. This was going nowhere.

"Do you remember about a year ago we went to a dance in Coventry and met two girls? Yours was named Grace I think. Anyway, we went back to their houses and stayed for a bit... literally! Well, it appears mine got pregnant and I now have a baby daughter called Jayne."

It was Tommy's turn to gasp, his mouth wide open in amazement.

"Bloody hell, there but for the grace of God go I."

"She's left me details of how to contact her if I want to meet and see the baby."

"So what are you going to do?"

"Right now I'm not sure; I need to think about it. I'll sleep on it and make a decision in the morning."

In fact he had very little sleep that night, going over in his head whether he should or shouldn't contact Isabel. Part of him desperately wanted to see the baby, but would it be right? He was attracted to Isabel of course, but the thought of settling down to marriage at his age appalled him.

He felt hands on him and thought he was being attacked, but it was only Tommy trying to waken him.

"Come on or we'll be on a charge, the rest of the lads are up and on the parade ground, inspection's in five minutes." Tommy's voice was urgent. He was dressed but wouldn't go without Mick.

Mick jumped out of bed and dressed in record time. Fortunately, he had cleaned his boots and belt the night before so all he had to do was dress and pick up his rifle.

They both ran out of the hut and into line just as the Sergeant Major appeared round the corner.

"Christ, you cut that fine," Tommy said after they had been dismissed.

"Sorry. I didn't sleep well last night, had a lot on my mind."

"Have you decided what you're going to do?"

"Yes, I am going to wait until this bloody war is over and then see them. I don't think it's fair to get involved and then if something happens to me they're back to square one. Anyway, with a bit of luck, the war will be over in twelve months and I can start a new life."

He wasn't to know that the twelve months would be four years.

CHAPTER ELEVEN

James had made a cup of tea for her and brought it to her bedroom. It was not often that she had a lie in, but last night's 'party' for Nigel had lasted longer than she had anticipated and the drink was taking its effect.

"Well Mum have you got over your 'surprise' yet?"

"Was I that obvious?"

"I'm afraid so, but don't worry, either Clare was too polite to say anything or she didn't notice."

"Did Nigel notice?"

"You're joking, he only had eyes for Clare. We might as well have not been there." He laughed at the memory. "Fortunately, Clare has all the social graces and made sure the conversation never lagged. I like her."

Jayne felt guilty at her behaviour. She was not at all racist and in fact had colleagues at the school both Asian and Jamaican, who had become firm friends; no it was just that she was expecting a young blonde, just like all the others had been. She had once asked Nigel if his girlfriends were clones because they all looked alike. He had not been amused and had not spoken for a couple of days.

"Mum, Mum are you still with us?"

"Yes. I was just thinking about last night. I feel rather embarrassed about my behaviour."

"Forget it. I'm sure Clare loves you. How couldn't she?"

Jayne smiled; James certainly had his father's charm... or bullshit!

Jayne dressed and showered and went downstairs to find a note from James on the hall table.

'Gone to library to investigate coat of arms. See you about lunch time. Love J.'

Trust him, she thought, can't wait to get on the case. There were other things on Jayne's mind and the locket was not high on her list of 'to do's'. Thursday was the day she did her weekly shop at the supermarket and it was already ten o'clock. Normally she would be out before nine.

James returned to the house just after lunch. He had grabbed a sandwich from the café next door to the library and had come home excited by what he discovered. He was surprised and a little deflated when he found his mother was not there. Hopefully she would not be long. Opening his briefcase he took out the notes he had made in the library and went over the information they contained.

When Jayne returned she found James sitting at the dining table with papers spread out before him.

"Had a good day I see," she said, pointing at the papers. "I know you're dying to tell me about it, but can you first help me put the groceries away?"

James hid his frustration and went to her car parked in the drive; the boot lid was already open revealing the numerous bags of groceries. Why, he thought, does she need all this food when there was just the three of them? It must be some sort of woman's logic!

The shopping was quickly stored away and, with a cup of piping hot tea in her hand, she finally sat down at the table.

"I'm all ears," she said.

"You wouldn't believe the amount of books there are on Heraldry. I spent at least an hour going through different volumes looking for something that would point me in the right direction. Finally, I found one book that showed the crests and mottos of the aristocracy, then had to wade through Earls and Barons before I got a match to the design on the locket. I found there were two that had the lions on either side of the shield, but one had two stripes on the shield itself, and the other had chevrons. It was the latter that most mirrored the design on the locket. It belonged to the Draycot family. The last Baronet had been Sir George Draycot who died in 1950 aged sixty-six. He had two daughters and no sons. There were no male relations alive and so the Baronetcy ended with his demise."

He stopped and took a drink of tea. Jayne sat, fascinated by what she was hearing.

"I then had to look for records of different Baronets and their families and eventually found the information I wanted. It gave details of family trees and a short biography of each one. Fortunately, the Draycot family line was not extensive. Sir George was the fifth to hold the title. The Draycots were unusual in that each son did not have any of his parent's Christian names, unlike most families who passed on one of their names to the next generation. George's father, for example, was Henry Charles and George's second name was David. As the locket had 'GD' written on the back of the picture, I thought it was safe to assume that George was the man we were looking for."

He took another sip of tea, but by now it was cold and he pushed the cup to one side.

"Do you want another?" his mother asked.

He shook his head.

"Having made up my mind I'd got the right man, I looked up his biography. It appears he was a bit of a high flier and in 1920 was being fast tracked to join the coalition cabinet of Lloyd George, but for some reason never actually made it. He remained an MP up until the end of the Second World War, then lost his seat in 1945 when Churchill lost the general election."

"That's all very well, but what has it got to do with the locket, or how did it come into my father's possession?"

"Patience, I haven't finished yet. I was intrigued by the paragraph saying that he never made the Cabinet, having been marked out for promotion. I decided that maybe he had done something wrong and there might be a report in the newspapers of the time explaining what it was. It was a bit of a long shot and it took me ages to wade through copies of *The Times* for that period, but eventually I got lucky. The paper had a regular column of what was happening on the Westminster scene. An article printed on 30th August 1920 said that Sir George Draycot would not be asked to join the Cabinet as it had been reported that his marriage was in some difficulty, due to an alleged affair with his children's nanny. His wife, of course, was standing behind him, but the local Tory party Chairman had hinted that he might be asked to resign. Apparently there were rumours that the girl was pregnant."

"So do you think Sir George gave this girl the locket and if so how did my father get it?" Jayne was totally puzzled and for all his efforts could not see where James's research had got them.

"Well maybe the baby was your father." James let the words hang in the air.

"Do you really think so?"

"Mum, I'm just guessing, I doubt there is any official record to prove it, but I could go to Worcester where Sir George lived and do a bit of digging. Who knows, I may find something. If we could find the name of the nanny it would be a start."

"You're really got the bug, haven't you?" she laughed. "Go on then Sherlock, see what you can find."

In spite of herself, Jayne was intrigued by the information that James had discovered. If James did find a connection and could prove that her father was the love child of Sir George, how would that help her discover what had become of him? Her mother had told her she thought that he had been killed in the Invasion of France in 1944, but had never seen his daughter. Jayne thought this strange, as by then she was three years old. Perhaps he chose not to see her because he didn't want her, but if that was so, why leave the locket to her, which must have been important for him to ask his friend to ensure she got it? The more she thought about it the more confused she became. A lot would depend on the results of James's investigations in Worcester.

CHAPTER TWELVE

Rumours were rife all over the camp. The talk of invasion, although officially banned, was the only topic in the mess room. It was an open secret that battalions in the North had been moved south and been assigned to camps around the Midlands and the Home Counties. The notices posted on the bulletin boards only stated that a series of manoeuvres were under way and everyone should be prepared to take part at a moment's notice. The C.O. had addressed the whole camp at parade and explained that they were making ready to fight to free Europe at the end of the year. No one believed him.

It was May 1944 and it was obvious, even to the ordinary soldier, that the summer was the ideal time to invade not the winter.

Mick and Tommy, like the rest of their group, had been on alert for the past two weeks with constant exercises dropped on them at a moment's notice. They were fighting fit and ready to go, that is until Tommy's accident. A supply of munitions had been delivered and, with two privates, they had been assigned to unload the trucks. Somehow, Tommy, who was behind one of the vehicles guiding it backwards towards the store doors, slipped, and the driver not seeing him, had reversed over his leg. The screams from Tommy as the wheels crushed the bones echoed around the camp. Mick was first to his friend and shouted to the driver to move forward to release him. Although a medic was with them in minutes, it was obvious that the leg could not be saved. Tommy's leg was amputated at the knee and for him the war was over, or at least the fighting. Mick was devastated, they had been like brothers and now Tommy wouldn't be at his side when the actual invasion took place. They had always looked after each other and Mick felt lost without his friend. Tommy was told that he could be invalided out of the army altogether, but persuaded the C.O. to give him a desk job; he still wanted to play a part, however small.

The news they had been waiting for came on the morning of June 5th. The brigade would be moving to the coast ready for the 'big push'. Tommy of course could not go and Mick had sought him out to say goodbye, possibly the last time they would meet.

For the last few days Mick had been thinking of the daughter he had never met. Had he done the right thing in not seeing her? It was three years now and the war was not over; in many ways it was only just starting. He had often thought about calling in to see Isabel, but each time he convinced himself he should wait and now it was too late; tomorrow, he was sure, would be the big day.

Mick had risen early having decided to ask Tommy to let his daughter know if anything happened to him.

History had repeated itself. Mick's mind went back to when he was sixteen. He had left school and was working in his father's garage as an apprentice mechanic. He was an only child and it had been understood all along that he would work in the business which, although not large, had given the family a good living. Even as a boy he had always helped in the garage and was a natural.

Mick and his father were more than just father and son, they were pals, and working in the garage was what he had always wanted to do. His mother was happy that the two got on so well and each day would make a packed lunch for them both.

It was early October and the weather had been damp and miserable. The side streets wore a blanket of dead leaves, which had been taken from the trees by the biting wind that was coming down from the North. Mick had noticed that his mother looked paler than usual, but assumed it was just the head cold that she had been complaining of for the last few days. That evening he was home before his father, who often stayed late to catch up on his paperwork. Entering the house he called out to his mother, letting her know he was home. Strangely she was not in the kitchen and he shouted again, this time a knocking sound from upstairs was all the response he got. Leaving the kitchen he made his way upstairs to the source of the knocking, which was coming from his mother's bedroom.

A gentle tap on her door was followed by a husky, "Come in."

"Are you alright, why are you in bed?" he asked.

"The doctor's been and said my cold is worse than I thought and I must stay in bed and rest."

"Don't worry, Dad and I can sort out dinner. I'll wait till he comes in and we'll rustle something up. Do you feel like eating?"

She shook her head.

"Perhaps some soup then?"

"Yes just a little, thank you."

Mick was worried; it was not at all like his mother to give in to a cold, so this must be more serious.

Over the next week his mother got weaker and weaker and was hardly eating anything. His father missed days from work to be with her and Mick felt isolated, unable to comprehend what was happening.

Each time he saw his mother she seemed thinner, as though she was slowly disappearing before his eyes. On the Friday, Mick came in from work as usual and his father, who had stayed home that day, came into the kitchen where his son was making a pot of tea.

"Mick, your mother asked if you could go up and see her."

"Of course, I was going anyway."

He entered the room and walked over to her bed, her face now white as alabaster.

"Mick, is that you?" her voice just a whisper. "There's something I want to talk to you about, come and sit close to me."

He pulled the chair close to his mother's bed and took her hand; it was cold and he could feel the bones of her fingers like the wooden hands on a marionette.

"There's something I've never told you but I think you have the right to know."

He looked puzzled, what on earth was she talking about, perhaps she was delirious.

"Your father is not your real father."

He started to interrupt, but she put her hand to his mouth, a sign to say listen.

"I am ashamed to say I became pregnant following a romance with my employer, where I worked as a nanny to his children and as a consequence had to leave my position and return home to my parents. You are the outcome of that affair. Please don't judge me too harshly because I really loved your natural father, but he was married and had a prominent place in society. If the affair had been made public it could have ruined him."

Mick said nothing, the shock having stolen his voice.

"The man you know as your father was an old school friend, who had carried a torch for me since we were young and when I returned home, he asked to take me out. When I confessed to him that I was pregnant, he immediately asked me to marry him and said he would say that you were his. Mick, what he did was to protect my good name and over the years I grew to love him, just as you do. I want you to promise me that you will always treat him as your father, he deserves that."

Mick's mind was spinning. He loved both his mother and his father and had always felt safe and protected in the family unit. Now he was totally confused as to who or what he was.

"So who was this man?" He could not bring himself to say 'father'.

"Sir George Draycot. He's an MP."

"Have you ever heard from him since you left your job?"

"No. When I left he gave me some money to help me start a new life, but I have never seen him since."

A tear appeared in the corner of her eye at the memory, clearly he had been the love of her life.

His mother coughed, the talking had been a strain and he passed her the medicine that sat on the bedside table. She drank it deeply and settled back onto her pillow.

Mick was not sure what to say. Not normally lost for words, the revelations had left him dumbfounded. He stood up deciding a tactical retreat would be for the best and less embarrassing. She did not let go of his hand.

"There's something else, Sir George gave me a memento when I left. Reach in that drawer and get it for me would you?"

He walked across the room to her dressing table and opened the top drawer.

"It's in a thin red box," she said in a voice hardly audible.

Mick reached inside the drawer and found the box and retraced his steps to the bed.

"Open it please."

The opened box revealed a gold locket on a chain, inside the locket was a picture of his mother. His curiosity took over and he lifted the picture out of its frame. On the back was written 'All my love GD'.

"I want you to have it, so that you will always remember me."

Her words hit him and a fear swept over him like a vast tidal wave taking his breath away. He was drowning and as the wave engulfed him he could see his mother on the shore waving goodbye. Gasping for air he wiped the vision from his eyes and looked at his mother lying motionless, her eyes now closed. He suddenly realised that there was no movement. The scream pierced the whole house and he crumpled at the side of the bed weeping uncontrollably.

His father rushed up the stairs and into the room, taking his son in his arms the pair stood there in their shared grief, both sobbing for the loss of their loved one.

The memory of that day had stayed with Mick ever since. At one fateful moment he had learnt of his illegitimacy and lost his mother, though strangely he had grown closer to Richard Furford who he had always known as his dad. Now he had a child of his own that he had not acknowledged, for fear of loving her and losing her.

With these thoughts in his mind he walked into the office where Tommy was as usual, in his wheel chair behind a desk stacked high with papers.

"Looks like the big day's arrived then?" Tommy said.

"Yes and I want you to do me a favour if you don't mind."

"You know you don't have to ask, anything for you mate."

"I want you to look after this locket 'till I get back, and if for any reason I don't make it, will you find Isabel and her daughter? I want Jayne to have it, it's a family heirloom."

"Come on mate of course you're coming back, you're indestructible." He gave a hollow laugh. They both knew the chances of not coming back were high.

Mick withdrew the box from his pocket and passed it to his friend. Without opening it, he wheeled his chair to the large safe that stood in the corner and locked it away.

"It'll be here waiting for you when you get back after kicking Hitler's arse."

They both laughed, every man in the army wanted to be the first to Berlin to perform that particular ceremony.

The friends shook hands, their grip held, not wanting to be the first to break the bond.

CHAPTER THIRTEEN

Jayne had looked forward to the school holidays. It would give her the opportunity to spend some quality time with her two sons, for although she saw Nigel every day, they were both busy and alternate weekends he would spend with his father. James, being away at university, she only saw during the holidays. Even then, there had been times when he had made arrangements to go skiing or deep sea diving with his college friends. She didn't really mind, but often felt a little neglected, so the eight weeks off at summer would be the time when they could get together.

It was not quite working out as she had planned. Since Nigel's birthday she had hardly seen him. He would pop in and out, spend a few minutes with her and then go again. It was obvious that Clare was now the centre of his world and he had all but moved in with her. Jayne was happy for her son but secretly felt that he was too young for a serious relationship, especially as he would be starting at Loughborough in September. The other worry she had was that Clare, at twenty, was two years older and certainly more sophisticated. She had a job in advertising and had her own flat; it was easy to see the attraction, apart from the obvious!

At least James was at home and his newfound desire to track down his long lost grandfather was his primary interest. She had to smile to herself as he showed more curiosity than her. Although she was intrigued she nevertheless thought that it was pointless. After all, it was assumed he had died in the war, for if he had not he would have found Tommy and got the locket back. The solicitor had said that Tommy had been asked to pass it on in the event of Mick not returning.

Having spent the weekend visiting his father James was raring to go. He planned to visit Worcester and see if he could find any information about the Draycots, especially relating to the period in 1920 when Sir George was hoping to get into the Cabinet.

"Mum, can I borrow your car today? I want to do some ferreting in Worcester and I have a suspicion I'm going to be dragged back and forth whilst I'm there."

Jayne reached into her handbag and withdrew her car keys.

"Make sure you drive carefully. I know you, you drive like a madman." She smiled as she passed the keys to him. "Have you got your note book and magnifying glass?" she teased.

"Ha, ha, very funny. You just wait. If I come back and tell you you're a duchess will you still be laughing?"

"Heaven forbid!" she replied.

James kissed her goodbye, promising to be back in time for dinner that evening.

She settled herself down in her favourite armchair to read the days papers, but could not help wondering if anything did turn up it would probably lead to a dead end and they'd be none the wiser.

James arrived home just as she was laying the table for the evening meal.

"I was wondering if you'd make it or not," she said as he pecked her on the cheek.

"Would I miss your hotpot? I don't think so."

"Well, what have you discovered?" In spite of herself she was curious.

"Patience, Mother. Let's have dinner first then I'll show you the fruits of my labour, I think you will be impressed. In fact I'm tempted to take up investigative journalism after this." He was joking but obviously pleased with himself.

The meal was quickly disposed of and pudding was put on hold. She cleared the table to enable him to spread his notes out, as he had done after the visit to the library, and was disappointed when all he had to show for his day's work was a small notebook.

"Are you sitting comfortably? Then we'll begin." He smiled to himself as he mimicked the words the narrator used on his favourite children's television programme when he was a small boy.

"Yes... yes... get on with it," his mother said impatiently.

"Come on Mum, indulge me, I'm enjoying this."

"Fine, but it had better be more exciting than the Magic Roundabout!"

"Right, well my first stop was the Manor House that had belonged to the Draycot family. Unfortunately I drew a blank immediately. The lady who answered the door informed me that the Draycots had sold the property years before. She had bought it from the people who in turn had purchased it from the Draycots. My next call was the local newspaper, *The Courier*; they were very helpful and let me go through old copies of the paper. I particularly wanted to see if there was anything relating to the rumour of Sir George's infidelity. I spent ages trawling through past copies until eventually I found an article by a young reporter by the name of Jeff Lloyd. The guy had done a couple of pieces in the gossip column. Firstly, he had reported that Sir George had failed to get the promotion to the cabinet that he was expected to have been given, and that the chairman of the local Conservative party had recommended that he should have the whip withdrawn. Sir George had survived a vote of censure, having vehemently denied the rumours of an affair with his children's nanny." He broke from his story. "Any chance of a drink Mum, this is thirsty work?"

Jayne pushed her seat back and went into the kitchen, returning with a bottle of beer.

"Carry on, I'm fascinated," she said as she passed him the bottle.

"Thanks... now where was I...? Oh yes I remember. Two days after this piece appeared in the paper, the same reporter wrote in his column that Florence Cowper, nanny to Sir George and Lady Draycot, had resigned from her post, adding that he was sure that it was pure coincidence that Florence was the same nanny at the centre of the rumours. Our friend, Mr Lloyd, must have had a mischievous nature, but nothing further appeared, either denials or confirmation, of his implications. So I now knew the name of the nanny, but had no proof that she was indeed pregnant and no idea where she went to. Of course all this had happened so long ago, there was no one currently working at the paper who went back that far."

"So that's it. We still don't know anything really." Jayne could not hide her disappointment. She had listened fascinated to her son's account, but they were no further forward.

"You're so impatient. I don't give up that easily. I admit I did think I had reached a dead end though. I told the receptionist at *The Courier* that I was doing a project for my university course. It was on aristocratic titles that had disappeared due to having no male heirs, hence my interest in the Draycots. She had asked her manager if I could look at the records and they had been very helpful. I think she could see the disappointment on my face when I handed back the old copies I had been looking through. I told her that there used to be a reporter by the name of Jeff Lloyd working for the paper, who seemed to know a lot about the Draycot family, but I expected that he was no longer alive. To my surprise she knew him, said he was a legend and had worked up until he was seventy. He now lived in an old people's home and by all accounts was, at ninety-three, still as bright as a button."

"So how does that help?" His mother could not see where this was going.

"I have an appointment to see him next week," James said triumphantly.

CHAPTER FOURTEEN

Mick had not slept well; the thought of the impending invasion had played on his mind all through the night. They had travelled down to the coast the day before and camped near the beaches. Before they had left camp his captain had called him in to tell him that he had been promoted to sergeant and would be in Lieutenant Faraday's platoon. Of course he had been pleased with the promotion and, like the rest of the men, was glad the waiting was over, but his emotions were mixed. Part of him was excited that at last they could get to grips with the enemy and show Hitler just what the British were made of, but he had to admit that he was afraid. He just couldn't understand why. This is what everyone had been praying for, the chance to show the world that we were still a great nation and would not be beaten. However, deep down he was scared. He knew he must hide these feelings; he was a sergeant and men even younger than he would expect him to show courage.

His platoon was assembled at 5.30 am; they had been told that they would embark at 06.00 hours. Everywhere he looked men were scurrying about, officers barking orders, vehicles being shunted into line awaiting their turn to load onto the ships that would take them to the Normandy beaches. They made their way to the troop ship, crammed together like sardines, thousands of men, tanks, Jeeps, armoured personnel carriers, all the paraphernalia of war. He made sure all the men in his platoon were accounted for and reported to Lieutenant Faraday.

Faraday was only twenty and looked even younger. He had a fair complexion with red hair, freckles and a slight frame and seemed totally out of place amongst all these testosterone charged soldiers; but he was an officer and the men would follow him wherever he led.

The ships slowly left the safety of the harbour and made their way through the choppy waters out into the channel, each man alone with his thoughts, some smoking, some chatting non-stop, even some cracking jokes, each dealing with the tension in his own way. The journey lasted two hours and, as they neared the coastline of France, they could see puffs of smoke rising into the sky where shells had burst from the guns on the mainland. The landing craft were lowered and platoon after platoon scurried down the ladders, quickly filling the boats that would take them on the last lap of this journey into the unknown.

Mick made sure the men in his platoon were all together in the second craft, each had his rifle ready in his hand, all filled with anticipation. For some strange reason the fear had left him, to be replaced by a burning desire to kill the enemy he had never seen. He looked at his men and saw fear in some eyes and hate in others, he knew he would have to try and set an example to those who were scared, to show them that they would win. He had not come all this way to die on a beach in northern France.

In no time he felt the bump as the landing craft hit the shore and the quartermaster blew hard on his whistle, as the front of the craft was dropped open for them to disembark.

The beach, codenamed 'Sword', was littered with coils of barbed wire placed by the Germans as the first line of defence, and small parties of men with cutters were already hacking their way through to provide a path for the rest of the troops.

Mick was right behind Faraday and shouted for his men to follow them through. All around them shells were landing, kicking up huge eruptions of sand as they detonated. Screams from dying and wounded men pierced the air, to be mixed by a cacophony of officers shouting instructions. Those who had been first through the wire had then taken up positions behind any clump of cover they could find and were firing inland, scattering bullets in the hope that some would find their targets.

He checked the platoon; thank God they had all made it, so far. They dug in and waited for the Beach Master to decide when they could move. The waiting was intolerable, everyone wanted to push on, not be stuck on a beach where they might be picked off by enemy aircraft. Mick looked down the beach and saw to his horror that the tide had turned and was slowly, inextricably coming in, reducing the area of beach available as each wave got closer.

"Sir, look at the sea, the tide's coming in, we need to move." His voice was urgent but controlled.

"I can see it, but we can't move until the Beach Master gives the signal." Faraday knew that soon he would have to make his own decision or they would be trapped by the rising waters.

The two men looked at each other but nothing more was said, they had their orders. Fortunately the dilemma was resolved. A loud whistle from the right and orders shouted through a loud hailer told them to move forward inland and on to higher ground. Shells were still dropping all around them, but no German soldiers appeared as they dug in. They had been hours on the beach and although only yards in land, had a foothold. They made camp and distributed a little food whilst the trucks and hardware were brought off the beach.

It was then that Mick, having checked on his men, realised that they hadn't come through unscathed. Two men were dead and another three were wounded. The medic had patched them up and at least they were able to walk.

Mick walked back to the beach and saw the carnage on the sand. Bodies lay where they had fallen, water lapping over them by the incoming tide. Some Jeeps and trucks were overturned and useless, blown up by the shells. However, the majority had survived. He wondered how the rest of the invasion had faired, the Americans, Canadians and other British regiments. There were four other beaches he knew, codenamed Utah, Omaha, Juno and Gold; he prayed they were as successful as Sword had been.

Faraday had been with the captain to get their orders for the next phase. He called Mick to him and relayed the instructions. They were heading for Caen, which was the largest city in northern Normandy. According to the intelligence reports, it was heavily fortified and the headquarters of the Germans in the area. Their platoon was to act as the rearguard when they made the advance. He had managed to obtain a Jeep and told Mick he wanted him to pick a reliable driver. Mick was to accompany him in the Jeep and they would ride 'shotgun'.

The men had dug hastily excavated trenches and settled down for the night; the next day was going to be hard going with the move on Caen.

A strange stillness hung in the air, interrupted by the odd thump of a shell landing in the distance. It was difficult to sleep. Mick had posted sentries and seen that all the men were as comfortable as possible in view of the conditions. One private had joked that it was as good as Claridges and, for a moment, laughter replaced the sound of death.

The sun dawned on an eerie peacefulness, the soft breeze brushed through the adjoining cornfield like the waves on a golden lake. All around men were stirring and cooks were distributing meagre rations and mugs of tea. It seemed odd that, looking to the south, all that could be seen were fields, but turn around and the scene was of khaki uniforms and all the paraphernalia of an army bent on revenge.

Once the platoon had eaten and drunk their fill of tea Mick reported to Lieutenant Faraday.

"All present and correct sir."

"Good man Furford. Have you got us a driver?"

"Yes sir, Private Jenkins."

Faraday nodded his approval. He left Mick to get the platoon into the trucks that would take them to Caen and went to Captain Thompson for a final briefing before they set off. Once all the men were settled in the trucks Mick and Jenkins went in search of the Jeep. By the time they came back Faraday had returned and was waiting for them at the back of the column. The radio crackled by Mick's side and he passed it to Faraday, knowing it was the signal for the column to move out. One by one the engines of the trucks stirred into life and like a giant snake slowly moved forward, the Jeep keeping station a hundred yards behind the last vehicle in the convoy.

The day was bright and clear with not a cloud in the sky and the convoy bumped along the country road; the troops in the trucks singing to keep their spirits up. They had been travelling for about an hour and had just driven past a small village where the locals had waved at them, thanking them, in their broken English for coming to their rescue, when it happened. From nowhere the sudden scream of aeroplane engines filled the air, followed by the staccato of machine gun fire as bullets ripped into the leading trucks. Men were jumping from vehicles and diving into the bushes that lined the road in an effort to escape the rain of death that was sprayed down upon them.

Faraday shouted for the driver to get closer to the convoy so that they could be with the platoon. The driver put his foot down just as the second wave of planes came above them. The bullets ripped through the windscreen killing Jenkins instantly. The Jeep careered off the road and into the ditch, turning over before hitting a tree. Men from the trucks in front had seen the crash and ran back to check on the occupants. They pulled Faraday's lifeless body from the wreckage; although not hit by any bullets, a large shard of glass from the broken windscreen had pierced his heart. Before they had a chance to go back to the Jeep for Mick, the petrol tank erupted and engulfed the vehicle in flames. No one could have survived the heat from the explosion. The men were ordered back to their vehicles, the planes now dots on the horizon, and the convoy regrouped to resume their journey.

Somehow Mick had survived. When the Jeep was first hit and veered off the road, it had hit a rock before turning over into the ditch and his body was catapulted out into the field. He had been knocked unconscious by the impact and the rescuers, not realising, had assumed he had perished in the explosion. He lay there unconscious for the best part of twenty-four hours and, when he eventually came round, was shivering with cold, the damp invading his limbs, the battledress little protection against the elements. He tried to move but nothing seemed to work, there was no feeling in his legs or arms and panic seized him with the thought that he might be paralysed. After a while he managed to move his fingers and slowly the feeling came back into his hands and arms. He rubbed his body to generate some warmth but the effort was tiring him. He looked around and wondered where on earth he was. He must be on manoeuvres somewhere, but was it Yorkshire or Warwickshire, he could not tell. Why wasn't Tommy there to help him? Tommy was always with him, they were mates. He tried to sit up but could not and after a couple more attempts he collapsed drifting off into unconsciousness again.

They found him still asleep at about mid-day. Rene and Jules had been out to repair a tractor for the local farmer and had noticed the burnt out Jeep in the ditch. They would have passed by without another thought if Jules had not seen what appeared to be something shining in the field by the side of the road. They had walked over to find that it was the reflection from the sun shining off Mick's watch. Rene, who was the older man, at first thought it was just another body killed by the attack on the convoy; there were plenty more scattered on the road. Then he noticed he was breathing. The two men gently sat him up, causing him to cry out in pain.

"Monsieur, Qu'est-ce que vous eprouvez? Pouvez-vous vous deplacer?" Rene looked down at him hoping he could understand.

Mick was awake now but could not understand what on earth they were saying. He seemed to remember they had been given some lecture on French and German back at the camp, with a few useful words they might need, but was this French or German and was this all part of the exercise to make it more realistic?

"Sorry mate, you'll have to speak properly I don't know what you are talking about."

The older man pointed to his legs and made a walking movement with his fingers.

"Oh I see... my legs... no I can't move them." Obviously they had been instructed not to speak English. He shook his head and pointed down.

The two men looked at each other, said something incomprehensible and, having decided on their course of action, took up a position either side of him. They linked their hands together; one pair under his thighs and the other pair across his back, to form a human armchair, and slowly lifted him off the ground. The pain flooded his body as they moved him and he passed out again.

"We need to get a doctor to him as soon as possible or all our efforts will have been in vain." Rene was stating the obvious and his young assistant could see by the grey lines etched on the Englishman's face that they might already be too late.

CHAPTER FIFTEEN

It had been a week since James had made his first visit to Worcester and now he was preparing for his appointment with Jeff Lloyd, the old reporter from *The Courier*. James was not quite sure how to approach the old man, so decided to use the same story as he had done at *The Courier*, that he was doing research into inherited titles that had been lost due to the lack of a male heir.

His appointment was for eleven but he arrived with fifteen minutes to spare, aiming to create a good impression with the older man for his punctuality and politeness.

The receptionist showed him into the day room and asked him to take a seat whilst they told Mr Lloyd that his visitor had arrived. The room was about forty feet square, light and airy, with floor to ceiling windows on the wall overlooking a neatly laid out lawn with box tree borders. The room was furnished with a number of easy chairs and coffee tables, with a large table at one side and a half a dozen dining chairs neatly slid under it. In the centre of the windows were double doors that led out onto a small paved patio with steps leading down to the lawn. The sun was shining and already some of the residents were sitting at the few tables on the patio chatting or, in some cases, taking forty winks. Not everyone had ventured outside even though the day was warm; some of the frailer ladies were sitting in armchairs in the day room, either knitting or reading. James noticed that of the residents that he could see the majority were ladies, outnumbering the men by at least three to one. It struck him as strange that nobody seemed to take any notice of him and carried on their routine as though he was invisible. He picked up a magazine that was lying on the coffee table next to him; it was six months out of date. It was like being in a doctor's waiting room!

An elderly gentleman, slightly stooped, walking with the aid of a stick, came up to him. He was smartly dressed in flannels, blue shirt and a yellow cravat. Although his face was lined, he had a good head of white hair and one would have put him in his early eighties.

"Mr Harris?" The older man held out his hand.

James stood up and took the man's offered hand, he was taken aback by the powerful grip and was glad he had grasped deeply into his palm.

"Mr Lloyd, thank you for seeing me." He pulled a chair next to his own for him to sit down.

"Well, young man how can I help you? You mentioned on the phone you were researching the Draycot family. I am afraid I only know of the last baronet, Sir George Draycot. He was our local MP when I was a lad about your age. I don't know if I can tell you very much that you can't find in the library."

James immediately liked the man; he was warm, easy going and had a twinkle in his eyes, with a little upturn at the corner of his mouth that made everything about him appear positive.

"Mr Lloyd…"

"Please call me Jeff."

"Jeff, I have a confession. I was not sure if you would see me, so I said that as part of my degree I was looking into hereditary titles. I am actually interested in finding out about Sir George's nanny, who I believe resigned at about the time there were rumours of an affair." He looked guilty and a little ashamed that he had sought to dupe this kindly old man.

Jeff did not show any sign of displeasure, on the contrary he was intrigued.

"So why are you interested in the girl?" The roles had been reversed and it was now Jeff Lloyd who was conducting the interview.

James felt he could trust the ex-reporter and decided to tell him the whole story. Jeff sat there as James explained about his mother being born during the war and having never met her father, then out of the blue receiving a locket with a picture of a young woman and a message signed GD. He went on that he had discovered that the engraving on the back was in fact the coat of arms of the Draycot family, how he had visited *The Courier* and had read the articles that Jeff had written, but the trail had gone cold, hence today's meeting.

The old man smiled, his eyes twinkled more brightly than ever... he was hooked!

"Do you have the locket with you?"

James reached into his inside pocket, pulled out the box and passed it to Jeff. Having opened the box he took out the locket and unclipped the fastening to reveal the picture.

"That's Florence Cowper and no mistake. She was beautiful, you can see why the old bastard had it off with her." He chuckled at the memory.

James was shaking with excitement. "You remember her then?"

"Oh yes I remember, in fact I interviewed her. I'd done a piece about Sir George missing out on promotion to the cabinet and had tried to find out about the rumours of an affair, but they closed ranks and wouldn't talk to me. Then within a few days it was announced that the nanny had resigned. They thought that everything was nicely covered up, but what they didn't know was that Laura, my girlfriend at the time, and Florence had become friends some months before. Laura went round to Florence in her digs and asked her why she had resigned. At first she wouldn't say anything, only that she wanted to go home to her parents. However, after a bit of persuasion and a couple of glasses of sherry she opened up to Laura telling her everything. She was pregnant by Sir George and, to save his career, had agreed to go back to her home in Wolverhampton and keep quiet about the baby. He had promised her that in a year, once all the fuss had died down, he would divorce Lady Draycot enabling them to marry. He had generously paid her a year's wages to help her 're-settle'. When Laura told me all this I went round to talk to her and tried to persuade her to let me publish the facts, but she was adamant that nothing should come out. I told her that it was doubtful she would ever hear from Sir George again, but it was no good, she was totally in love with him. I asked her what she would do and she said she would go back to her parents. Her father was the headmaster of the local grammar school. Laura kept in touch with her for a while and I understand that her parents persuaded her to marry just before the baby was born. Her new husband was an ex-school friend who'd always carried a torch for her and willingly accepted the baby as his. Laura lost contact, although I think she said that the baby was a boy. Rather ironic that Sir George's only son was born out of wedlock and the title could not be passed on.

"After her marriage I wanted to run a story about the affair but was warned off by my editor. It would seem that the 'Tory mafia' had got to him."

James could not believe his luck. He had not expected to get so much information.

"You said your girlfriend kept in touch for a while, so she must have had Florence's address to write to her?"

"Yes, but if you're going to ask me what it is I'm afraid you're going to be out of luck. She wouldn't tell me in case I went after her, said she'd had enough problems without a bloody reporter bothering her. In fact we had a row about it and that was the end of our relationship." He smiled as the memory of his girlfriend drifted into his mind. "Bloody shame, she was a bit of alright."

James could not hide his disappointment; to have got this far and still not found the connection left him deflated.

Jeff saw the look on the young man's face.

"Would it help if I gave you the name of the man she married?" he asked teasingly.

"Do you know?" James could hardly contain himself.

"Of course," he laughed. "I managed to get that from Laura before she made me promise not to take it further."

"Well, come on then, what is it?" James had dropped his politeness in his anxiety to know.

"Furford, Richard Furford."

"Christ, my mother's father was Mick Furford; he must be the illegitimate son of Sir George." James could hardly believe what he was saying.

"Well that makes you the great grandson of Sir George." Jeff smiled. "I take it I have been of some help to you then?" The old man felt pleased with himself.

"Yes... yes... thank you for all your help. I will need to try and trace Mr Furford, but at least I've got something to go on."

"I might be able to help you there; although Laura would not give me an address she did let slip that the new husband had a business, a small car repair garage."

James wrote this last piece of information in his notebook. He stood up and shook Jeff's hand.

"Thank you again you have been really helpful."

"It's been a pleasure and please let me know how you get on I'd be very interested."

"I promise."

James left the old man sitting in his chair still with that mischievous smile on his face.

CHAPTER SIXTEEN

They had taken Mick back to Rene's house and, with the help of his daughter, had managed to get him upstairs into the bed. Giselle had been sent to fetch the doctor whilst the two men took off his wet clothes. His body was a deadweight and he had not regained consciousness. They wondered if all their labour was in vain and that perhaps he was already dead.

The doctor eventually arrived and was shown into the room, the two men leaving him alone with the soldier. It was twenty minutes before the doctor came down to join them in the kitchen.

"He seems to be suffering from concussion. There are no serious injuries, except for some minor bruising and lacerations which you would expect. You think he was thrown from a Jeep when it crashed and the injuries are consistent with that. I will need to examine him again when he comes round. In the meantime let him rest and when he wakes give him plenty of liquids. I expect he hasn't drunk anything for some time and will be dehydrated."

The doctor left and the two men went back to the workshop at the rear of the house. Giselle was left to keep watch over the Englishman.

It was evening and Giselle had prepared supper for her and her father. Giselle's mother had died three years earlier when the Germans had entered the village. Along with a number of women she had been at the kerbside as a column of trucks passed. Someone had thrown a brick at the windscreen of the leading truck and instinctively the driver had swerved, mounted the kerb and ploughed into the women, killing Giselle's mother and two friends. Giselle was only seventeen but was now the 'woman' of the house and looked after her father, who had never really recovered from the incident.

As they were about to sit down at the kitchen table to eat, Rene heard a groan from above and they both ran towards the stairs. Reaching the bedroom they found Mick trying to sit up but being too weak to make the move.

"Monsieur, s'il vous plait, il fait vous restez tranquille." Giselle reached him first and pushed the pillow under his back to give him some support. "Est que je peut vous preparer queleque chose a manger?"

Mick stared at her blankly, what on earth was she saying?

"Parlez-vous Francais?"

He stared at them without replying. Why were they keeping up this pretence of speaking some foreign language, and why was he in this bedroom and not either in camp or hospital?

Rene turned to Giselle. "I'll go and get the doctor. He speaks a little English, perhaps he can make him understand. Meanwhile try and get him to eat some of the soup you have made for us."

Rene hurried out of the house and Giselle went back to the kitchen and fetched a bowl of hot vegetable soup. Mick tried to hold the spoon she offered him but his hand was shaking too much. She held the bowl close to his chin and fed him like a child.

The warm liquid permeated his body and he felt some strength coming back to his arms, but still could not feel any movement in his legs.

The soup was quickly finished and he looked at this beautiful girl who sat by his bedside, wanting to thank her but not knowing how to.

She had long dark hair that was naturally curly, with blue eyes that seemed to shine like sapphires. Her complexion was soft and creamy and he guessed from her boyish figure that she was quite young. Her breasts were small and pert; in fact she was like an angel. Perhaps he had died and gone to heaven! He lay there with a silly smile on his face, not caring about the pain, just enjoying the vision in front of him.

The mood was broken by the sound of footsteps on the stairs and the voices of Rene and the doctor.

"Alors! You are awake, bon." The doctor in his broken English spoke as he approached the bed.
"Where am I?" Mick asked.
"Monsieur, you are in France. You have had the accident."
"France? How, why? How did I get here?"
"You are the soldier. You chase away the Germans. But please I need to test you."
"You mean examine me."
The doctor nodded his head.
"I can't move my legs and I can't remember how I got here, or anything come to that, except that I'm in the army and I thought in Yorkshire on manoeuvres."
The doctor looked perplexed. The Englishman was talking too fast for him to fully understand and he did not understand the words Yorkshire or manoeuvres. The doctor chose to ignore what had been said; instead he pulled the sheets back and looked at Mick's legs. There were no apparent injuries but Mick could not move them. He lifted one leg so that it was bent and tapped just below the kneecap but no response; he repeated the process with the other leg, still no response. He pulled the sheets back, then holding a small torch looked into each eye in turn.
"What is it Doctor?" Mick's voice was anxious.
"Monsieur, you have suffered from the head and lost the memory. Your legs have also lost the memory to work."
"Jesus, am I paralysed, is it permanent?"
"Mais non. You will get the legs better but it will take time, the head also, but when?" He gave a shrug of the shoulders to indicate that even he could not answer that.
For the first time in his life Mick felt despair. He was alone in a strange country, amongst people who he could not communicate with, and no memory of who he was or what he was doing there. All that he could recall was being a soldier in Yorkshire with his friend Tommy, everything else was a blank. Try as he might he seemed only to remember that one brief episode, it was as though he had been dropped from space into a tiny world that had lasted for just a few days. Panic gripped him, a feeling of being trapped, not being able to move, suffocating

and finally dying under this invisible weight that pressed down on his chest. He let out a piercing scream.

The doctor, who had been quietly giving Giselle instructions on how to try and get Mick to exercise his legs to speed their recovery, quickly moved to the bedside. Mick was trying to struggle, the pathetic movements having little effect, and the more he tried the more frantic he became. The doctor, realising the problem, gave him a sedative to relax him and he drifted off into a fitful sleep.

"He will sleep now for at least eight hours and rest is what he needs most. He also needs help trying to get his memory back. The brain is a strange thing and can play tricks some times. He will need to re-learn many things and slowly, hopefully, a trigger will open a part of his memory that is at the moment locked away." The doctor looked at Giselle. "If you can help him, I am sure he will make a full recovery in time."

"But doctor, I don't speak English and he obviously doesn't speak French. How can I help?"

"Then you must both learn together. I have a French/English dictionary that I can lend you and I will be calling in from time to time to check on him, so I can perhaps help when you are finding things difficult, but I warn you my English is not wonderful." He smiled at her as an uncle would to his favourite niece. He had known Giselle since he delivered her as a baby and was sure that if any one could look after the soldier it would be her.

CHAPTER SEVENTEEN

When James arrived home from his visit to Worcester the house was empty. A note propped up against the teapot in the kitchen read: 'Gone to grandma's... be back in time for dinner. It's cottage pie! Love Mum.' He grimaced; she knew he hated cottage pie. He took the notepad that had been left on the table next to the note and quickly scribbled a message for his mother. 'Have had a call from Jack, he wants to go out for a curry, probably be back late, don't wait up. Love J.'

Although that was not technically true, he was sure his friend Jack would be only too willing to rescue him from the clutches of the cottage pie and go for a meal. He dialled the number. The phone rang out and after the fifth ring he started to panic that maybe his friend would not be there to provide his excuse. Finally, Jack's voice came on the line and quickly agreed to the subterfuge.

It was only four o'clock but James decided to wash, change and leave the house early, before his mother returned, in case she came up with the bright idea of inviting Jack to come round and share the delights of her cottage pie.

He took some time to shower, feeling the stinging rays of the hot water soothing the stiffness in his body caused by the cramped space in his mother's car; it had not been designed for a strapping six foot rugby player. As he stood there, the streams of water cascading over him, he thought of his meeting with Jeff. What a remarkable man to have the clarity of memory at the age of ninety-three and to be so full of life. He resolved to keep in touch with Jeff because he felt a kindred spirit with this man, in spite of their age gap.

The weather was fine, so he decided to walk the half mile to Jack's house and then they could call a taxi from there to the restaurant. After such a successful day celebrations were in order, so there was no point in taking the car.

Jayne arrived home at about five thirty, not realising she had missed her son by only five minutes. Seeing the car in the drive she bounded up the path, trying, but with little effect, to quell the excitement of finding out what he had discovered that day. She opened the door and shouted out that she was home. To her surprise there was no immediate response, so walked through the hall into the kitchen, still no sign of James. Then she noticed the note sitting next to the one she had left for him. Her disappointment was palpable, not with him missing out on her delicious pie, but that she would have to wait until the morning before getting an update on his 'detective' work.

Feeling deflated she went into the living room and poured a gin and tonic. It was barely six p.m. but what the hell! On an impulse she picked the phone and dialled Debra's number.

"Hi! Are you doing anything tonight? Do you fancy going out for a meal?"

"Oh Jayne, I'd love to normally but I can't tonight, got a date with this hunk I've met. He's taking me to that posh French restaurant that you went to for Nigel's birthday."

Jayne replaced the phone. It seemed her luck was out everywhere, even Nigel had hardly been seen since the night of his birthday. She settled down to a night in front of the television, even the cottage pie temporarily forgotten.

She woke next morning with a splitting headache the result of too many gin and tonics on top of half a bottle of Chianti. At least she would never be an alcoholic, the feeling next day was so bad that she always abstained for at least a week after a session like the night before. When she had finally showered and dressed, the process taking twice as long as normal, she made her way downstairs to find James in the kitchen.

"You look rough, good night?"

"That's not a very nice way to greet your mother," she chided. "As everyone had deserted me, I resorted to my old friend 'Bill Bottle' and we had a very pleasant evening. Unfortunately, he was not to kind to my head and now I'm paying for it."

James laughed; at least his mother had a sense of humour, although he did feel a twinge of guilt about sneaking off, but he knew she would soon forgive him once he relayed his latest news. He made her a cup of tea and some toast and she settled down to listen.

"As you know, I had an appointment to meet the ex-reporter from *The Courier* at the old people's home he now lives in. You just wouldn't believe how sprightly and switched-on he is, for ninety-three he's amazing. Anyway, he recalled the incident with Sir George being overlooked for promotion and the resignation of the nanny soon after the rumours of his 'affair'. He had tried to interview the nanny but she refused."

"It sounds as though you had a wasted journey then." Jayne looked disappointed.

"Mum, don't be so impatient, let me finish. Jeff had a girlfriend at the time who knew the nanny and, with the help of a few drinks, got the full story. The nanny was pregnant with Sir George's child and had agreed to leave his employ and return to her parents in Wolverhampton. And this is the best bit, Sir George promised that once all the furore died down he would divorce his wife and marry her! The nanny was totally in love with Sir George and believed him. Jeff's girlfriend had made him promise not to print the story."

"So where does that take us? The nanny goes back to Wolverhampton, has a baby, so what?" Jayne felt frustrated; it seemed that it was another dead end.

James smiled; he was saving the best till last.

"Jeff asked me why I was interested and I showed him the locket. He recognised the picture straight away, said her name was Florence Cowper... Sir George's nanny."

His mother started to interrupt him but he held his hand up to stop her.

"Jeff's girlfriend kept in touch with Florence after she had returned to Wolverhampton, and it turns out that her parents convinced her that Sir George would not keep his promise. Instead an old flame from her school days offered to marry her and bring the child up as his own... and that man's name was

Richard Furford and the baby was a boy." James's voice was triumphal.

His mother just stared at him trying to take in what she had just been told. Was it really conceivable that her father, Mick Furford, was in fact the illegitimate son of Sir George Draycot?

"Do you think from what you've discovered that my father is Sir George's son?" Jayne looked quizzically at James, waiting for his reply.

"Yes Mum, I do, I definitely do. What we must try and find out now is what happened to him. Grandma says she thinks he was killed in the war, so there must be some way of checking. The Ministry of Defence must have records. Jeff also told me that Richard Furford ran a small garage in Wolverhampton and that might be worth checking on. I would think that Richard and Florence would be dead by now, but there might be other members of the family alive. Who knows, you might have some step brothers and sisters." He laughed at the suggestion but could see his mother was not at all amused.

"Perhaps you should talk to your gran and tell her what you have found out. She may be able to give you some idea of his regiment, so that you can chase up the records."

Jayne, as always was being practical, although she had to admit to herself a little excitement about what James had discovered.

James had the bit between his teeth and decided to ring his grandmother straight away. He went into the hall to phone her but was back a few minutes later not looking too happy.

"What did she say?" Jayne enquired.

"Not a lot really. She was surprised by the connection to Sir George but couldn't help much about what regiment he was in. All she knew was that he was based at Bramcote and although she had tried to contact him he had never called back. She never saw him again and just assumed he had died during the invasion. It's going to be like looking for a needle in a haystack trying to trace him from so little information."

Jayne put her arm round her son's shoulders. "I'm sure if anybody can find the truth you can."

CHAPTER EIGHTEEN

Mick woke to the sound of birds chattering outside his window, the sunlight sending a shaft of golden light through the gap in the curtains. He could now sit up by pushing his hands on to the bed and shuffling his body backwards, but there was still no response from his legs. It had been the same routine for nearly two weeks and after each struggle to even get to this position, the fear swept over him, that despite what the doctor had said, he might never walk again. In the first few days Giselle had tried to help him sit up but he had roughly pushed her away, determined to maintain his independence. He could see that his actions had hurt her, she had been so kind, but he had to do it himself.

He lay there trapped in his useless body and worse, with no memory other than a small window of time. His only recollection was being in an army unit on manoeuvres with his friend Tommy. The memory only covered about three days, everything else was blank.

Giselle had been wonderful, not only had she nursed him and dressed the superficial wounds that he received from the crash, but sat listening to his incessant questions, although not understanding most of what he was saying.

The doctor had been as good as his word and brought her his French/English dictionary within a few days of his initial visit. It was a long-winded process for her to look up every word he said to her and she had to motion him to slow down and say one word at a time. They both became very frustrated and Mick would slip into a morose state and clam up. After a week they were getting nowhere and Mick feared that his frustration would get the better of him, and he would lose her support altogether.

It was Giselle who came up with the solution. She had laboriously prepared her idea, translating words from French to English, in bold capitals.

As always she gave a gentle tap on the door before entering his room and, without waiting for an answer, walked in, crossed the room and drew back the curtains. The sunlight flooded the bedroom bringing the whole room to life.

"Bonjour monsieur, comment ca va?"

His blank look the normal response to her cheerful greeting. She took the papers she was carrying, from under her arm and, laying them on the bed, placed one sheet in front of him. On the paper she had written:

| BONJOUR | GOODMORNING |
| COMMENT CA VA | HOW ARE YOU |

He smiled. He made a gesture with his hand to indicate he wanted to write and she nodded and fetched a pencil from the table.

VERY WELL THANKYOU He wrote the words in capitals just as she had and passed her the paper. Taking the dictionary from her pocket she looked up the words and wrote the French translation next to them.

TRES BIEN MERCI

They both grinned at each other like school children at their first class. She had found a way to break down the barrier. It would be long-winded and laborious but at least he would not feel so isolated and desolate.

Pointing to herself she said, "Je m'appelle Giselle, en Anglais my name is Giselle. Vous, vous appellez Michel, en Anglais your name is Michael." She held up papers she had found in his tunic which gave his name, rank and army number and pointed to his name written on them.

The second sheet of paper had a list of objects with their English translation.

LA FENETRE	THE WINDOW
LA PORTE	THE DOOR
LE CHEZ	THE CHAIR
LE LIT	THE BED
LE TAPIS	THE RUG

LE TABLEAU	THE PICTURE
LE VERRE	THE DRINKING GLASS
L'ASSIETTE	THE PLATE
LE FOURCHETTE	THE FORK
LE COUTEAU	THE KNIFE
LA CUILLERE	THE SPOON
LE PAIN	THE BREAD

As she went down the list saying the word slowly, she would point to the window or door or chair. After each word he repeated the French translation. She seemed pleased with him and he in turn was pleased with himself, for a brief moment the hopelessness that pervaded him forgotten. Giselle held up her hand to indicate that they should stop and he looked quizzically at her. To his surprise she turned and left the room. The door closed but immediately there was a knock and she reappeared.

"Bonjour Monsieur, comment ca va?"

He realised straight away what she was doing.

"Er..Tres bien, merci," he responded.

"Tres, bon… very good."

He beckoned her to bring the dictionary to him, and flicking through the pages found the word he wanted.

"You," he pointed to her, "tres jolie… very pretty."

She blushed, not used to being given compliments.

They went over the list again and again until he held is hand up.

"Enough, I'm tired," and held his hands to the side of his head and closed his eyes to indicate sleep. She nodded her understanding and left the room. It was a start, a small breakthrough, but hopefully as time passed, they would be able to understand each other and she could learn about this stranger who had entered her life, in fact was taking over her life.

Each day they would spend an hour in the morning and an hour in the afternoon on their lessons. It was a joint venture because they were both learning the other's language at the same time, though it was soon obvious that she was the quicker and more responsive one. The morning session consisted of learning new words and the afternoon a memory test. Mick thought it strange that he could remember nothing before the accident, but everything that had happened since.

Within a couple of weeks he could count up to a hundred and knew the days, weeks and months of the year. They had agreed that they would always try and speak in the other's language, but at times his frustration got the better of him and he would revert to his mother tongue. Giselle's patience was boundless and she would let him finish his rant then calmly go over again, slowly, what he was trying to say.

By the beginning of August he was putting together short sentences with the odd English word thrown in. As always she would look up the word in her dictionary and make him repeat what he wanted to say in French. She seemed to be able to converse much better in English than he could in French, but never let him off the hook, insisting on keeping to their agreement to speak in the other's language. What he didn't know at the time was that she spent extra time practising whilst he rested. Her father was beginning to feel neglected and had at times wished he had never rescued the Englishman.

August the 25th 1944 was a big day for two reasons. As usual he had woken up and gone through his routine to get himself into a sitting position. Having got comfortable he would try and wiggle his toes to see if there was any response. He looked hopefully, but with little expectation, down at his feet. Then suddenly he noticed a movement or was it just a trick of the light?

"Giselle, come here quickly!" he shouted at the top of his voice, forgetting their pact that he must always speak French.

Her feet pounded the stairs as she ran in response to his shout. The bedroom door was flung open without the customary polite knock.

"What is wrong? Are you hurt?"

"No, no... but I think there is movement." He pointed to his toes.

An audible sigh of relief escaped from her mouth as she sat on the side of the bed.

"Can you lift the foot?"

"No, but are the toes moving?" His brain was sending messages to his feet, pleading, begging them to move.

"Yes... .yes." Giselle gave an excited cry. "They are moving, only a little, but definitely moving."

Tears ran down his cheeks. It was as if a weight that had pinned him down, was being lifted from him, releasing him from his self imagined prison.

She looked at him, realising the enormity of this small movement and what it meant. Reaching into the pocket of her dress she pulled out her handkerchief and gently wiped the tears from his face. He reached up and held her hand and for a moment their eyes met, each looking deep into the soul of the other. Neither spoke as he pulled her to him and his lips searched for hers. He could feel her breasts rising and falling against his body as she made no move to break the embrace.

Finally he moved away, looking embarrassed.

"I'm sorry, I hope I have not offended you."

"Offended? J'e ne comprend pas." She moved to the table and picked up the dictionary, finding the word, she smiled. "No you do not offend me."

He smiled back relieved that the moment would not be spoilt. The problem was he wanted to kiss her again! It was as though she could read his mind and leaning forward, she kissed him hard on the mouth. His arms instantly wrapped around her, not wanting to ever let her go.

That morning's lesson took on a completely new light and they both found difficulty in concentrating, preferring to deviate from her set plan and concentrate on translating words like love, embrace, kiss and touch.

He needed his midday rest more than usual, but unlike most days when he would drift of to sleep, could not settle. The excitement of knowing that there was movement in his legs, coupled with the other stirring he had felt, had brought new life to him. Eventually he did doze off, a silly smile playing on his lips as he did so.

It was afternoon when Giselle came bursting into his room for the second time that day.

"Michel, Michel wake up Paris has been liberated." She was an excited schoolgirl who had just learnt that all her exams had been passed.

Mick stirred. "What's all the noise about? What do you mean Paris is liberated, from what?"

She had forgotten that Mick did not remember that there was a war being fought all over Europe to defeat Nazi Germany, and that he had once been part of it. Since her father had brought Mick to the house they had never talked about the war, for in truth she had not wanted him to realise how and why he was there, for fear he would go. Now she would have to explain her excitement at the news having taken over.

"You recall telling me that all you can remember is that you were in the army training with your friend?" He nodded. "Well the British and Americans invaded France to fight the Germans who had invaded our country. You were part of that invasion but had an accident when your Jeep crashed. I think your army friends thought you had died when the Jeep blew up, but Papa found you in a field next to the road the next day."

Mick sat there in silence, he remembered nothing of the incident or being part of any invasion.

"So are we winning?" he asked. In truth he really didn't care, all he wanted was to be with Giselle.

She laughed, "Yes we are winning, de Gaulle our leader, has accepted the German's surrender in Paris and we have a French government again. Now the Allies are pushing the Germans back across the border, soon it will be all over." The consequence of what she was saying suddenly hit her. With the war over Michael would leave!

CHAPTER NINETEEN

James had gone out early to visit some of his old friends from the secondary school, deciding to take a break from his 'investigation'. Jayne was busying herself cleaning the house and with the vacuum cleaner full on did not hear the telephone when it first rang, switching the machine off she just reached it before the caller hung up.

"Hello, can I speak to James please?" It was a man's voice, but not one she recognised.

"I'm sorry he's out can I take a message?"

"Oh... er... yes, can you ask him to call Jeff please, he's got my number."

Before she could say any more, or ask if she could help, he put the phone down. How rude she thought. The name Jeff didn't register as any friend that James had talked about and he sounded a lot older than any of her son's contemporaries. She made a note on the kitchen pad so that she would not forget to tell him when he returned. As it happened he did not return until late that night and Jayne was sound asleep when he came in.

Next morning Jayne was woken by a knock on her door and James asking if he could come in. He was already dressed and had made her a cup of tea.

"That's very welcome, but why? Have you done something wrong?" She was laughing; remembering that when James was young, if he had got into trouble he would always try and win his mother round with a good deed, before confessing his misdemeanour.

"No, nothing, don't be so cynical, I just thought you'd like to be pampered. I won't do it again if that's all the thanks I get." He feigned a hurt expression and they both smiled. "I saw your note in the kitchen to ring Jeff; did he say what he wanted?"

"No, in fact he was rather short, put the phone down before I could ask him if I could help. Who is he anyway?"

"He's the reporter from *The Courier*, you remember, the old man who was so helpful about the Draycots."

"Oh yes, I never thought about him. Never mind, have you rung him yet?"

"I think it's a bit early to be ringing an old people's home don't you?"

She looked at the clock, it was only eight thirty.

James left his mother's room and she got out of bed, showered and dressed. By the time she had put on her make-up for the day and gone down to the kitchen, it was nine fifteen. James put his fingers to his lips indicating to her to keep quiet as he was about to phone Jeff.

He got the receptionist who said yes Jeff was up and was in the day room and she would send someone to fetch him. James settled down to wait; the day room was at the other end of the building from the reception desk, so he knew it would be a few minutes before Jeff reached the phone. After a while Jeff's familiar voice came on the line.

"Hello, Jeff speaking, who's that?"

"Good morning Jeff it's James, you rang me yesterday whilst I was out. Something you wanted to tell me?"

"Oh... yes... James, thanks for phoning back. After your visit the other day it set me thinking about old Sir George and a couple of bits of information that I don't think I mentioned to you."

James's ears pricked up, this could be interesting. "Go on then don't keep me on tenterhooks."

The old man chuckled down the phone; he liked the boy but could not resist playing with him a little. He paused as though collecting his thoughts before finally speaking. "Well I remember Laura telling me, before we had that blazing row, that she had secretly spoken to Sir George and told him that Florence had told her what had happened, but had sworn her to secrecy. She told Sir George that she felt he had a right to know that he had a son and gave him the boy's name, and that Florence had married a local businessman in Wolverhampton."

James whistled. "So Sir George knew of his son then."

"Yes, and there's something else that came back to me after your visit. Sir George died in 1954, we did an obituary in the paper, but I got a tip off from a clerk in a solicitors' office that there was a problem over the will." He paused to let his words sink in, knowing that James would be champing at the bit wanting him to continue.

"What problem?" James could not wait.

The old man chuckled, enjoying himself.

"Lady Draycot had died the previous year, so his two daughters were the next of kin and stood to inherit, not only the family home but, a considerable amount of money. Sir George had many directorships and was a wealthy man. Both daughters had married and no longer lived in England. The eldest had married an Australian and moved to Sydney to live. The other daughter's husband worked for an investment company and had been moved to head their American arm, so lived in New York. When they came over for the funeral and to sort out their father's affairs the problem came up."

"What problem? James was getting frustrated; he just wanted Jeff to cut to the chase. Not being interested in the family background.

"Patience, I'm coming to that. My informant told me that when the will was read there was a bequest of £500,000 for one Michael Furford, who's last known address was Wolverhampton. He had actually named him as his son."

"Crikey!" James could hardly contain his surprise.

"I thought that would make you sit up. Needless to say the two daughters were shell-shocked as they obviously had never been told of their stepbrother. They immediately contested the will, but were informed by the solicitors that it was perfectly correct and legal. I wanted to run a piece in the paper about the will and the 'bastard' child, but again my editor suppressed the story I wrote. It would seem, even from the grave, Sir George wielded some power."

"But what happened to the money?" James's mind was racing with all the possibilities that this information had thrown up.

"I understand that they tried to trace Michael, and although they interviewed his stepfather they were told that he had never returned home at the end of the war, having been listed as 'lost in action presumed dead', but there was no proof either way."

"So what happened to the legacy?"

"That's the interesting bit, apparently in cases like this the inheritance passes to the other legatees, but if the original inheritor turns up then they have to pay him. I spoke to my own solicitor and he told me that in such cases they usually advised their clients to take out an insurance policy, so that if by some remote chance there was a claim they would be covered. Although this was fairly costly, it was paid out of the estate, there would still be a net benefit."

"Wow, so if Michael Furford is alive then he can claim £500,000 pus interest I suppose?"

"I would say yes he could, but the question is, if he is alive does he know the legacy exists?"

"You don't happen to remember the name of the solicitors do you?"

Jeff chuckled again, he really was enjoying himself.

"I guessed you would want to know that. They are Hodgeson Smyth and Co., still going in the high street in Worcester, though the main partners at the time have probably retired by now. Is your mother going to claim her inheritance then?"

In all honesty it had not crossed James's mind, even if she wanted to she had no proof of her lineage.

"James are you still there?"

He had gone quiet, letting all the information sink in.

"Yes, sorry, I was just thinking, it's quite a surprise."

"Look I'll leave you to it, but let me know if you find out any more, I can't deny I'm intrigued, in fact it's really brightened my day."

They said there goodbyes and James promised to keep in touch.

Jayne had been standing by the side of the phone, but had only been able to hear one side of the conversation and was confused. What was all this about half a million pounds? She wanted to ask so many questions but sensibly curbed her excitement, knowing that James would explain everything to her.

"Let me get you a drink and you can tell me what all that was about."

James sat down at the kitchen table, his mother opposite him and proceeded to relate his conversation with Jeff. She sat there without interrupting but with an ever-increasing look of incredulity on her face. Could it really be true that her father was entitled to all that money, and if he was dead was she the next of kin, and more to the point, would she have any legal claim? Strangely the thought of maybe inheriting such a large amount was not what was uppermost in her thoughts. The more that James found out about her lost father the more she wanted to meet him. There were so many questions going round in her head, but the one that was coming to the front of her mind was 'do I have any siblings'?

"James you must go to Wolverhampton and see if you can trace Mr Furford."

"You must be a mind reader; I was just thinking the same thing."

CHAPTER TWENTY

From that day in August when he first had some response in his toes, each day after, he would try and move his legs and feet. At first it seemed that only the toes would ever move and despair would creep over him, but it did not last long, once Giselle entered the room and gave him her trademark smile, his frustration disappeared.

Since that first kiss he had felt a reason to go on, when the doubts came he would think of her and knew he could overcome anything.

The weeks dragged by with little noticeable improvement. He was bedridden and totally dependent on Rene and Giselle, although she seemed to enjoy his need of her. His French was improving and he could even hold a conversation of sorts with Rene, who spoke no English whatsoever. The doctor still called regularly to check on his patient and brush up on his own English.

On his latest visit he had again checked his reflexes and surprised Mick by saying he felt there was a big improvement. For the life of him Mick could not understand how, but at least it was encouraging. Before leaving, the doctor gave Giselle a list of exercises that she should help Mick with, to improve the response in his useless limbs.

So now the days took on a new regime of exercises, language lessons, exercises and language lessons. By the end of each evening he was exhausted.

Giselle was tireless, nothing was too much trouble and, better still, if he did well he was rewarded with a kiss, chaste at first but as the weeks passed the embrace was held for longer and longer.

The day came when he could actually move each foot, not just the toes and with each day's exercise a tingling sensation grew along his legs. There were days when he lost the sensation, then he feared that he would not recover, but Giselle would not let him drift back, threatening to withhold her favours if he didn't keep going. She was his rock.

Winter had come and gone and the trees and bushes were taking on a green glow as the buds began to open. Mick was now able to sit in a chair next to the window. Getting into the chair was the difficult part and it took both Giselle and her father to lift him in. Rene would patiently spare time to perform the manoeuvre each day before he left to go to his workshop, and return him to the bed when he arrived home. The two men had grown closer together from this bond that had been forged through adversity, the one the dependent, the other the provider. As Mick's mastery of French improved so the bond grew stronger. They had even started to play drafts during the winter evenings, a state of affairs that did not go down too well with Giselle, who wanted to keep him to herself.

Being able to look out of the window seemed to open up his world and gave him renewed energy to get better. Since the doctor had told him that eventually the feeling would return to his legs, he had determined to walk again as soon as possible. It was not unusual for Giselle to find him crumpled in a heap by his chair, having tried to stand unaided. Unlike the early days, he was not daunted by any set-back and would persevere, although needing Giselle to be there.

By April the days were warmer, flowers were bursting into life, and so was he. At last he could now stand without holding on to anyone or anything. It seemed that good news was all around. Giselle would keep him up-to-date with the news of the Allies' progress. They were now on the edge of Berlin; it would soon be over.

May the 8th 1945, the Germans finally conceded defeat and the war in Europe was officially over.

Rene came home early that day and surprised Mick when he came into his bedroom. He had a full bottle of brandy in his hand, which he had obviously been saving for just such an occasion. Mick was in his chair by the window but managed to stand up to greet Rene. The two men embraced. Giselle had by now accepted the friendship between the two men and was no longer jealous.

"Mon brave this is a very special day, the war is over, you do not have to worry."

Mick was not worried! He knew nothing of this war that they talked of. As far as he was concerned it never happened, his world consisted of this room, Rene and most of all Giselle.

Rene poured the brandy into the three glasses he had brought.

"Salute, to France, liberty, oh and England, of course." Rene held his glass high and both Giselle and Mick chinked their glasses with his.

Mick sat down before his legs gave way, the brandy was too good to risk spilling! He looked from father to daughter and saw the relief in their eyes. They had had come out of a long dark tunnel and could now rebuild their lives, just as he was rebuilding his.

CHAPTER TWENTY-ONE

The news that the war was over was being celebrated in every house, shop, office and most of all the public houses in the country. Isabel had finished her shift at the Morris Engines factory at Courthouse Green and had rushed home to celebrate with her mother. The war years had taken their toll on her and although still only twenty-six, she looked nearly thirty-six. For the last two years she had worked at the factory in the accounts department, having left the ambulance service because the hours were difficult to combine with bringing up a toddler. Her mother had been a godsend, but she too was getting on and a spirited child was more than a handful.

Isabel had started as a clerk, but had an aptitude for figures and very quickly was given more and more responsibility. The only man in the department was the accounts manager and he was in his early sixties; all the rest of the team were either young women or older spinsters. The manager had taken a shine to Isabel and she knew it. This was an opportunity that was not to be missed, and she made sure that if there was something special he wanted done, she would volunteer for it. Fortunately she was popular with the other girls and apart from a couple of the older ones, who had been there for years and felt their noses were being pushed out, no one was envious. The manager came to rely on her more and more and now she was his unofficial deputy.

Jayne was nearly four, walking and talking and into everything. Her grandmother doted on the child and had been instrumental in her pre-school education. She would read to her everyday, so much so, that the child knew some of the words off by heart, even though she couldn't read them herself. Each night after work Isabel would catch the bus home in time to spend an hour with Jayne before she went to bed. At weekends she would devote herself solely to the child to give her mother a break. Mrs

Brown was fiercely proud of her daughter with the way she had accepted her responsibilities, and would offer to baby sit each Friday, so that Isabel could have a night out with her friend Grace. It was an offer that was greatly appreciated but not always taken up. War-torn Britain had not been a place for enjoyment.

Tonight was different, on her way home Isabel had called in at the outdoor and bought a bottle of gin, her mother's favourite tipple, and as soon as she entered the house, took it out of its brown carrier bag and waved it at her mother.

"Get some glasses Mum we're celebrating."

Jayne stared up at her mother, not understanding what all the commotion was about. Isabel swept the child up into her arms and squeezed her.

"It's a good day Jayne," she said in answer to her daughter's puzzled look. "We've won the war."

"What's a war?" Jayne asked.

"Not very nice." Her mother replied, laughing at the little girl's innocence.

Mrs Brown came back in from the kitchen, two tumblers in her hand.

"Make it a double, Isabel, I think we deserve it don't you?" She was laughing as well.

The past was now confined to history, a black period, one which could not be forgotten, but not one to be remembered. The two women drank their gins, draining them down at one go.

"Fill them up again, will you love? Let's have a toast to all those that have made today possible and who won't be coming home to celebrate."

Isabel did her mother's bidding and the glasses were replenished. They raised their glasses and in unison said. "To our fighting men."

"I wonder if your Mick made it?"

"I don't know Mum, I don't even know if he went to France, he never contacted me, remember."

"I know, but I think you should go back to that camp and try and find out."

"Yes I suppose you're right, but there's no point yet, the peace has only been signed today."

They both laughed at the absurdity of the situation, the gin beginning to take effect now.

Isabel bathed Jayne and put her to bed. She wanted to make sure her daughter was safely tucked in before the alcohol started to take full effect.

Mrs Brown had her faithful wireless playing in the background, but tonight all normal programmes had been superseded by constant updates on the armistice. The two women relaxed for the first time in six years, the fear, the apprehension, the worry, lifted from their shoulders. Now they could rebuild their lives, lives that had been on hold during the uncertainty of those dreadful times.

Mr Churchill's voice could be heard in the background thanking the soldiers for the magnificent victory, thanking the British people for their stoicism and thanking God for delivering us from this unspeakable hell.

"Good old Winnie; I knew he would pull us through," Mrs Brown said, rather loudly.

"Mum not so loud, you'll wake Jayne up." Isabel giggled; she too was beginning to feel the effects of the gin.

Churchill droned on in the background, warning everyone that the task was not yet complete, and the war in the Far East must be ended as soon as possible for the world to be truly free.

Isabel replenished their glasses again and proposed a toast, "To Winnie."

Mrs Brown chinked her glass against her daughter's, rather harder than she meant to and a little of the liquid spilt onto the floor.

"Whoops... can't waste it can we luv?" Her giggling had now turned to laughter as she sat down with a thud into her favourite chair.

By ten o'clock the bottle lay empty, Mrs Brown snoring in her armchair and Isabel was finding it difficult to focus. She managed to rouse her mother enough to get her on her feet and, with an arm around her for support, slowly they made their way upstairs. Mrs Brown revived enough to kiss her daughter goodnight before flopping onto her bed. She was asleep almost as soon as she hit the pillow and Isabel, being in no state to help her undress, threw a blanket over her and left. Within minutes she too was in bed fast asleep.

Jayne, as always, woke at seven and could not understand why the house was so quiet. Usually her mother or grandma could be heard as they made breakfast in the kitchen, but this morning all was silent. She felt frightened by this strange stillness all around her. She jumped out of bed and ran to her mother's room. She could see the outline of her mother's body in the bed but no movement. She tried to shake her but there was no response. Turning from her mother she ran into the adjacent room where her grandmother slept. She too was not stirring either. Jayne felt panic grip her, why didn't they wake up?

Mrs Brown kept a large jug filled with water in her bedroom, in case she needed a drink in the night. Jayne thought that a drink of water would be just what she needed to help her wake up, so pulled the stool close to the table that held the jug and standing on it was now tall enough to reach the handle. Even with both hands the jug could not be lifted and at the third attempt she lost her balance and fell, still gripping the handle of the jug. The jug crashed to the floor soaking her with water but luckily not hitting her as it shattered into pieces on the wooden boards. She let out a piercing scream as the shock of the cold water hit her, but at least it had the desired effect of waking both her grandmother and her mother, the latter running into the bedroom fearing a catastrophe.

Jayne sat, soaking wet, tears streaming down her cheeks. She knew she had done something wrong and was expecting to be scolded.

"Oh darling... it's okay... Mummy's not angry. It's my fault I should have been awake." Isabel cuddled her daughter ignoring the wet nightdress until the sobbing subsided.

Mrs Brown had also been woken by the scream and quickly realised what happened, obviously little Jayne had been frightened and scared that breaking the jug would spell trouble. She smiled down at her granddaughter.

"Don't worry, Grandma's not mad at you, it was an old jug anyway." The lie fell easily from her lips. "Isabel, you'd better get ready for work or you'll be in trouble, I'll see to Jayne's breakfast."

"Thanks Mum, I don't know what I would do without you." She leant forward and kissed her mother's cheek.

There was no time for breakfast, not even a cup of tea, as she ran down the stairs and out onto the street to catch the bus.

She need not have worried as it seemed everyone had been celebrating. Apart from Mr Davis her manager, she was the first to arrive at the office, and even he was in a particular happy mood that morning, not once admonishing the girls as they slowly drifted in.

The initial euphoria died down over the following months as slowly the nation tried to get back to normality. The peace brought its own problems, with rationing, and returning soldiers vying for the few jobs that were available. Isabel was thankful that she had made herself indispensable at the factory. The company had returned to making engines for motor cars, but unfortunately the demand was slow with the economy stagnating under the weight of national debt that the war had incurred. Lend-lease had been the saviour of Britain in the war years but now it was crippling the economy. It was pay-back time. As the older women in the office left they were not replaced, but at least there were no lay offs.

In the September Jayne started school, she would not be five until the following July and was the youngest in her year, just scraping in before the cut-off point. Isabel managed to wangle a few days' leave from work, so that she could take her daughter to the school each day for the first week of the new term.

Her daughter was growing up before her eyes. It seemed like only yesterday that she had been on her cousin's farm giving birth. Her thoughts inevitably turned to Mick and she wondered where he was or whether he had even survived the war. She had secretly hoped in those first few months that he would come and see her and Jayne, but it never happened and she had assumed that he didn't want the responsibility, some men were like that.

In truth she did not really know much about Mick, after all, they had not been in love but had shared a moment, a need. That moment had resulted in their daughter and for that she would be eternally grateful. It was strange but she felt he was different, caring, and compassionate and could not reconcile those feelings with the fact he had never made contact. She decided she would take her mother's advice and visit the camp in Bramcote to try one last time to find him.

On the Saturday, with Grace again by her side for moral support, she caught the bus to Nuneaton. The two women again found themselves outside the barrier that barred the entrance to the camp. The soldier on duty left his sentry box and walked across to where they stood.

"Can I help you ladies?"

"Yes I would like to speak to an officer please, I'm looking for a soldier." Jayne was more confident than the first visit.

"Well you've come to the right place we've got hundreds to choose from." The sentry chuckled at his own joke. Isabel turned a bright shade of red, she had not realised how stupid she must have sounded.

"I'm sorry Miss, didn't mean to embarrass you, please wait and I'll ring through."

The soldier returned to his box and after a couple of minutes poked his head round the door.

"There'll be someone along in minute to take you to the captain."

The two friends waited. It was as if it were only yesterday that they had stood in the same spot waiting to be escorted in to see the officer in charge. This time they did not wait long before a young private appeared and beckoned them to follow him. They were shown to the same office as before, but this time the desk sergeant was different and so was the officer to whom they were introduced.

"How can I help you?" The captain was about the same age as Isabel and had a strong Scottish accent.

"I am enquiring after a soldier, a Corporal Furford, I wondered if he was here or if…" her voice trailed off.

The officer understood, nobody wanted to mention the word… died. He called to the sergeant in the outside office to come in and asked him to look through the records for a Corporal Mick Furford. The sergeant left the room but reappeared within a couple of minutes.

"There was a Sergeant Mick Furford who was with the invasion party on 'Sword', last record of him was in Faraday's group heading for Caen. If you remember sir, Lieutenant Faraday was killed by enemy fire when his Jeep was shot up, the report said that Furford was with him but no body was found. He's listed missing presumed dead."

Isabel felt her heart sink.

"I'm sorry Miss, was he a relation?" The captain's voice was kind; he had been the messenger of bad news many times before.

"Not exactly, we weren't married but we have a daughter whom he has never seen." She could not hold back the tears at the thought that now he would never see her. "Thank you captain you have been most helpful." She managed to get the words out in between the crying.

Grace put her arm round her friend's shoulder and the two women left the room.

"Christ! How many times have I done that and how many more times will there be?" the captain asked himself, sotto voce.

She had only known Mick for a few hours, yet they had a bond that even in death could not be broken.

CHAPTER TWENTY-TWO

Although the feeling had returned to his legs and he could walk again, he still had no memory of his life before he met Giselle and Rene, save for a brief window on being with a friend called Tommy, and that was like a scene from a play with no beginning or end.

From what Giselle had told him he was lucky to be alive, for the war which had passed him by had claimed thousands of lives and nearly his.

Now France, like other European countries, was waking up to the post war realities of reviving a stagnant economy and rebuilding a shattered country.

Rene ran a small workshop repairing farm machinery and servicing tractors, with the help of Jules, a young man barely eighteen, who he had been given a job purely because he was the son of a friend. The lad was not academic but worked hard and had slowly picked up the skills that Rene passed on to him, the skills that he had hoped to one day pass on to a son of his own. During the war he had struggled to barely make a living, but now things were picking up and he had expanded by repairing the farmers' cars as well as their machinery.

Now that Mick was not restricted to his bedroom, he wanted to get out and about to learn more about his adopted country. He had never been one for sitting around and felt frustrated again.

"You are never content are you?" Giselle asked, as they sat at the breakfast table.

"You don't understand, I've been trapped in my bed for months, hardly being able to move, I need to do something." He looked into her eyes and could see the sadness in them, as though he had reproached her. "Giselle," his hand reached out to hers, "without you I would never have survived. I don't want to leave you... ever... but I need to do something... do you understand?"

The smile came back to her lips. "Yes I think I do."

He pushed his chair back and moved around the table and she stood up to face him.

"Giselle, I love you."

He took her into his arms and pulled her tightly to him and gently kissed her. Her body quivered as he held the kiss, not wanting it to end.

"And I love you too," she said, as he finally released his grip around her waist.

They were both smiling now, holding hands, saying nothing just looking into each other's eyes. He felt as though he owned the world. For months he had wanted to tell her just how he felt but had been too frightened of rejection. Yes she often kissed him, but he had not been sure if the kisses had been caring or loving, and now he knew.

"Can we tell Rene?" he asked hesitantly.

"Of course, but I think Papa already suspects." She laughed at his worried look. "I do not think he will mind even though you are a foreigner."

She was teasing him but it didn't matter, nothing mattered as long as she loved him.

He helped her clear away the breakfast plates and washed them while she dried and put them into the cupboard.

"Can we go for a walk? It's a beautiful day and I want to tell the world how much I love you."

"Will your French be good enough do you think?"

"Of course, I've had the best teacher in the world."

"Come on then, where would you like to go first?"

"To your father's workshop, there's something I need to ask him."

"Oh what is that?"

"Be patient, my darling, you'll soon see."

It was a bright, warm day, befitting the mood he was in, as they left the house and walked the half mile to the centre of the village, where Rene had his workshop.

Rene's workshop was small and had just about room enough to hold two vehicles. Unfortunately, only one vehicle at a time could be worked on in the cramped space. At the back of the workplace a small office had been erected which held a desk and a lone chair. On the desk was a telephone and a large notepad, obviously used for taking clients' names and addresses. Mick knew that all the office paperwork, bills and invoices, was done from the house, usually by Giselle. Next to the office on the back wall a large bench had been fixed to the brickwork. It held a couple of vices and numerous tools strewn carelessly on its surface. Mick felt strangely at home in this place, almost as though he recognised it. It was an odd feeling that he could not understand.

When they walked in Rene turned, looking up from the car he had been working on.

"What brings you two here?" he asked.

"I would like to speak with you." Mick said the words formally as though at an interview.

Rene gave a half smile, he had become friends with the Englishman over these last months and they had never spoken in the formal manner that he was now using. He thought he knew what was coming next.

"I wondered if you would consider allowing me to work for you. I would like to repay you in some way for your kind hospitality. You saved my life and I owe you a debt. If I could work here with you… for no wages of course… I would feel…."

He did not finish the sentence.

"My friend you owe us nothing. You and your countrymen rescued us from the Germans, it's the least we could do. You are my guest for as long as you want to stay."

He could not have imagined that Mick would ask that question, he had thought of something entirely different.

"Rene you are too kind and I thank you for your generosity." He was still using his formal method of address and even Giselle was wondering where it was all leading too.

"As you know, I can't remember anything before the accident, but for some strange reason this place has a familiar feel about it. Can I ask what you are doing?"

"But of course. This car has had an accident and the back axle needs to be removed and replaced, look I'll show you."

Rene lay on his back and Mick lay next to him. The car had been jacked up so that the two men could slide underneath. The damaged axle was almost off and it would take only the removal of a few nuts to completely free it. Mick instinctively picked up a spanner and deftly removed the nuts. Rene slid out from under the car.

"But you know exactly what to do, were you a mechanic?"

"In truth I don't know, but I am sure I can do the things that are required to repair your machinery. Will you let me work with you? I have a feeling that there will be other things I can do. I just need to see them."

"Michael," he had always called him Michael as that was the name written in the papers they had found in his tunic, "consider yourself employed, but you will not work for nothing. I will make a bargain with you: I will pay you a wage and you will pay me a rent, the difference is yours to squander." He laughed at his own joke as he held out his hand.

Mick took his hand and shook it vigorously.

"You just hired a new assistant. There is one other thing I wanted to ask you. I would like your permission to marry Giselle." The last words, though still formal, came out in a rush and he stepped back afraid of the reaction he might receive.

There was no need for him to worry. This had been the question that Rene had expected from the beginning. However, Rene could not resist toying with him for a moment or two and he pretended to consider carefully the request. The waiting seemed to Mick like an eternity before Rene finally, and with a grave expression, shook his head.

"I am afraid you cannot marry my daughter…"

Mick's jaw dropped, this could not be happening, he had been sure that Rene would say yes.

"…until you have worked for me for at least…"

Mick looked at Giselle, she too was surprised.

"…a month." Rene burst out laughing, no longer able to continue the charade.

Giselle threw her arms around her father and kissed him.

"Giselle, I think we will need to take Michael to town to buy him some new clothes, I don't want my daughter to marry a man in a worn out old army uniform."

Mick looked from Giselle to Rene, he felt more contented and relaxed than he had done for a long, long time.

CHAPTER TWENTY-THREE

The weeks had flown by and soon James would be back at university, and this year Nigel would be starting his course at Nottingham. Jayne had to admit that she would feel a little lonely once they had gone. Although Nigel hardly spent any time at the house now that he had all but moved in with Clare, at least she had James for company.

Over the past few years she had never really thought about her father, being too busy getting on with her life as a single mother and teacher. The events of recent weeks made her wonder what would have happened if her father had survived the war. Would he have eventually come to find her? Her mother had never been bitter about him apparently not wanting to see them, but she could not help feeling a little resentment in the fact he had totally ignored her, at least that is how she felt until the locket came to light. She reasoned that he would not have made his friend promise to pass it on to her if he had not wanted some sort of contact. Now, following James's enquiries, there was a new twist to the tale and possibly an inheritance.

Something was nagging at Jayne; she did not know why but felt that her father had not died. She knew she had no facts on which to base this notion, but it was a feeling that would not go away. Her mother had told her that Mick was reported missing, presumed killed, during the invasion, but what if he had survived and come back trying to find her.

She was only six years old when her mother had married her first husband but Jayne hardly remembered him. He had been much older than her mother and she had never understood why they married in the first place. He had lost his wife and within a few months had married her mum. They had moved from Grandma Brown's house and gone to live in her new stepfather's house on the Tamworth Road, on the outskirts of

Coventry. It was much larger with four bedrooms and a separate dining room; to a six-year-old child it seemed enormous.

Harold Davies had been kind to her, but with his own children grown up and married themselves, was not used to small children and did tend to get a little irritable at times. It was a short lived marriage, however, for after only two years he suddenly died of a heart attack and Jayne found herself fatherless again. When Mr Davies died, Jayne's grandmother moved in with them, selling her house in Coundon; it was just like old times again. Years later Isabel had told Jayne that Mr Davies's children had been left half of the house in his will, and that to stay there she had to pay them off. Luckily, Grandma Brown's sale of her house provided enough capital to clear the payment.

Isabel had profited in two ways by the demise of her husband, not only did she inherit half the house, but was promoted into his job at the office where she had been his number two. Jayne remembered that since her mother had met and married Mr Davies, they enjoyed a better living standard and Christmas presents did not just consist of one toy, a few sweets and two oranges! In fact, for her eighth birthday her 'new dad' had bought her a bicycle, but sadly never saw her learn to ride it as he had his heart attack just ten days later.

Jayne's mind recalled those early events in her life, realising that if her real father had returned and gone to Donnington Road to try and find her, then he would have found them gone, and Grandma Brown had left no forwarding address.

"What are you thinking about? You seem miles away."

She had not heard James come into the kitchen and turned with a start when he spoke.

"You're not spending your inheritance are you? He chuckled not being able to resist the chance to tease her.

"Don't be silly," she said, blushing all same. "But I can't help feeling your grandfather never died in the war. Don't ask me why, it's just... I don't know... intuition maybe."

"Woman's intuition," he said rather grandly.

"We're more often right than we are wrong so don't be patronising."

"Well Madam Zelda what does your crystal ball say about Mr Furford of Wolverhampton?"

"Now you're just being silly, of course I don't know what you will find but I'm sure you'll find something."

"Now who's being patronising?"

They both laughed.

After a cup of tea and a scan through the day's newspaper, James collected his notebook, slipped it into his jacket pocket and scooped up the car keys from the hall table, before giving his mother a peck on the cheek to say goodbye. He was ready for Wolverhampton.

As he drove the car out of the drive he went over in his mind his plan of action. He had the address of Florence Furford nee Cowper that Jeff had given him, and had decided that would be his first port of call.

The journey took about three quarters of an hour to get to the town centre, and once there he pulled up outside a newsagents and bought a local A to Z. He took the map back to the car and soon found the address he had been given, which fortunately was only a few streets from where he was parked. With the map opened on the passenger seat next to him, he slowly made his way to the destination, glancing from the road to the map and back again as he drove. He drove down the road looking from side to side hoping there would be a garage with the name Furford in bold letters above it, but having reached the end of the street... nothing. He turned the car around and slowly retraced the route. On the first pass he had not noticed a large piece of barren land in between a row of terraced houses on one side, and a block of four shops on the other. Pulling up outside the shops he got out of the car and walked up to the second shop in the block which had a sign above it saying... 'IRON. MONGER' and underneath 'all hardware supplied here'. He smiled at the awful pun of the proprietor's name but thought if anyone knows who lives where I bet he does.

The bell clanged as he opened the shop door and a man about fifty, with long hair wearing a brown coat, appeared at the counter. He wore his hair long in the style of a pop star, but one who had not washed it for ages.

"Can I help you?" the man asked.

"I hope so, I'm looking for a garage owned by a Mr Furford, I was told it was in this street but I can't find it."

"Furford's Garage, yes you're parked outside it, or I should say where it used to be. It was burnt to the ground years ago."

"Oh." James could not hide the disappointment in his voice. "Did you know the Furfords then?"

"Not exactly, I am trying to trace some distant relations and I think Mr Furford was one of them." For some reason he did not want to explain to this man the whole story.

"Well I'm afraid you won't get very far here. After the fire Furford became something of a hermit. My dad said that he felt he had lost everything. His wife died years earlier from pneumonia and his only son never returned from the war, so he had nothing except his work. When the fire took that, he just gave up. I heard that he had a breakdown and died in the 'loony bin' sorry, I mean the mental health home."

"But wasn't the garage insured? Surely he could have started again?"

"Like I said he just lost interest. I suppose it was insured. I can ask my old man if you like."

"Could you? It might help me trace any other relations if I could find out who inherited his estate and the date he died."

"Look, leave me a contact number and I'll phone you when I've spoken to my dad."

James wrote his telephone number on the pad that the shopkeeper pushed towards him.

"Thanks for your help; I look forward to hearing from you."

As James walked back to the car he could not help thinking that he had reached the end of the road. Mick was the only son and if, as seemed likely, he was dead, then that was the end of the story. He could not help feeling that he had let his mother down, she had been so sure that he would solve the mystery.

"Well, what did you find out?"

James had hardly had time to hang his coat up when his mother posed the question.

"A bit of a disappointment I'm afraid. Mr Furford's garage burnt down years ago and he died not long after, apparently he had never accepted the loss of his wife and son."

Jayne looked disappointed; she had felt sure that James would bring back some information about her father, or at the very least his family.

"Did he have any other children?" she asked, although she knew the answer before James confirmed that Mick was an only child. "So that's it, a dead end... literally."

"Not quite. I asked the shopkeeper, who told me about the fire, if the place had been insured and if so what happened to the estate when Mr Furford died. He is going to ask his father and said he would ring me and let me know, so that might lead us somewhere but I'm not holding out much hope."

Jayne put her arm round her son.

"Cheer up. Look, from what you have found out we're related to a baronet and might even have a claim to an inheritance, and I still have this feeling that my father is alive, though why I feel this I've no idea."

James smiled. Trust his mother to look on the bright side; she always saw the glass half full not half empty.

"Come on Mum, let's eat out tonight... my treat."

Jayne ran upstairs to quickly change her dress and apply a dab of lipstick while James reversed the car out of the garage.

Over dinner they chatted about Nigel and Clare, university life, anything other than the locket and Mick Furford. That subject had dominated their lives for the last few weeks and it was refreshing to have a different topic of conversation.

On returning home Jayne checked to see if there were any messages on the answer phone. There was just one.

"Hello... James? This is Dave Monger. We met today at my shop. I've spoken to my father and he said that the garage was insured and it was all dealt with through Furford's solicitors, Davies and Renshaw of 21 Lower Street Wolverhampton. He died in March 1953... hope that's some help to you... bye."

"Well I suppose I'd better follow it up as we've come this far." He kissed his mother lightly on the cheek. "I'm off to bed to get an early start...'night."

CHAPTER TWENTY-FOUR

The wedding was not a grand affair but that didn't matter to Mick, he was just happy to be with Giselle. She walked into the tiny church on her father's arm looking radiant. Mick had Jules as his best man and the whole village as witnesses. The priest blessed them both and pronounced them man and wife. The ceremony was over in what seemed like seconds. There was no reception, instead the three of them went back to Rene's house and celebrated with a simple meal and copious amounts of red wine.

Mick had started work for his father-in-law to be, a month before as agreed. Rene could not believe how well Mick worked, it was obvious that he had been a mechanic before the war, he was a natural.

Before Mick joined him there were certain jobs that Rene would not undertake, preferring to stick to simple repairs and maintenance of farm machinery, but Mick was a wizard with anything mechanical, especially cars. After only a few weeks Rene had been persuaded to take on more work, and his reputation for quality was rapidly spreading in the surrounding area. They were working Saturdays and Sundays just to keep up with the demand. It was obvious that they needed more hands to cope and the little village workshop was bursting at the seams.

Mick was blissfully happy, he was doing something he loved, had a beautiful wife and was now fully recovered from his injuries; the only fly in the ointment was he still had no memory of his life before he met Giselle, but that was only a minor irritation in his new world.

They had been working at the repair shop almost without respite for the past six months, and even though they had extended the barn to take another 'car bay', it was clear that they would soon be letting customers down. Rene had been happy in the old days to just make ends meet, but he could sense that Mick wanted more.

After Sunday dinner he leaned across the table.

"Michael," he poured them both a glass of cognac, "I've been thinking."

"Congratulations Rene, do you want a prize?"

"Michael, please! I am being serious, do not make fun. I think that we must either expand the business or contract, we cannot go on like this or we will kill ourselves."

Mick wanted to say something but his father-in-law held up his hand.

"Let me finish. You have a gift for this work and I can see you are ambitious and not afraid of hard work, so I have a proposal. I have some savings which have grown considerably in these last months, and I suggest that we find some premises in Bayeux and open a proper garage repairers. In the city we will be able to attract more custom and especially the sort that have money. What do you think?"

"Rene, you know I love the work and I will always be grateful for the way you have supported me. It would be an honour to work for you in this new enterprise."

"But no my friend I do not want you to work for me, I want you to be my partner."

Giselle had been listening to the conversation from the kitchen and at this point ran into the room and threw her arms round her father.

"Papa, I love you. You're wonderful."

Mick sat there, his mouth open, unable to speak, he had not expected anything like this.

"Rene, you are too generous, I can't accept this, but I will willingly work for you in this new adventure."

"Well you must choose, but if you do not accept my proposal then I will contract the business and stay a small repairer here in the village, it's up to you."

"Michael you must accept, don't you see it's what papa wants for you, for me and for him." Giselle looked at her husband her eyes imploring him to say yes.

"Rene, what can I say, I am outnumbered two to one," he laughed. "Yes, yes, yes."

The three hugged each other, the bond now unbreakable.

"I have even thought of a name for our new enterprise, 'REMICH CAR REPAIRS', what do you think?" Rene asked.

Giselle grinned, she could see straight away how her father had amalgamated his and Michael's names to form the new name.

"Rene, I think you are a very special man, and I thank you and promise that we will be the best garage for miles." Mick held out his hand and Rene took it and shook it vigorously.

What Mick did not know was that Rene had already set about finding premises in Bayeux. The following Thursday they left Jules in the workshop and drove the ten miles to the city.

Just off the main street they pulled up outside a petrol station with a large building of about two thousand square metres behind it. The premises were boarded up and the petrol pumps padlocked. The agent was already there waiting with the particulars.

A small dapper man in a striped suit carrying a brief case came towards them as they got out of the car.

"Good morning gentlemen. Monsieur Martin, Monsieur Furford I presume?"

"Yes, have you the keys?" Rene wasted no time with the pleasantries, he knew they needed to get back as soon as possible or they would be working through the night.

The agent let them in through a side door. The workshop looked vast in comparison to the small workshop they were used to. They walked around the building, it had two pits for working under cars and four offices on a mezzanine floor at the front; it was perfect.

"Why is it all locked up?" Rene asked.

"The owner was in the Resistance and was caught by the Germans and shot, they closed it as part of their reprisals and it's been closed ever since. The owner's widow does not want it so she has been trying to sell it, but has had no offers up to now. I think she would take almost anything to get it off her hands."

"What do you think Michael?" Rene looked at his son-in-law but could see from the grin that spread from ear to ear exactly what he thought. "Please offer the lady seventy-five percent of the asking price to be paid in two instalments, fifty percent now and the balance in one year. I have the cash and will sign the contract immediately."

The agent looked surprised; he had almost given up on ever selling the property and was sure that the owner would accept the offer.

"Gentlemen I will speak to my client, immediately I return to my office and will contact you as soon as I have a decision."

They shook the agent's hand and he left the pair still gazing at the building.

"Rene, I think it's perfect, but can you afford it?"

"Don't worry, that is why I said we would pay the balance in a year, it gives you time to earn the money." He laughed at Mick's worried look. He had no worries as he was convinced that Mick would soon have the place buzzing.

The agent was as good as his word and phoned them that afternoon with the news that the widow had accepted their offer without any question. The contracts would be drawn up immediately and they could take possession once they were signed.

Mick was frustrated, things had moved so fast at first, but it was now two weeks after the initial visit and still they had not signed the contract. Rene was more relaxed, he knew that solicitors moved at the pace of snails. Finally, the formalities were completed and, borrowing a truck from a local farmer, they loaded up all their tools and workbenches and transferred them to the new site. Once the contract had been signed Rene had commissioned a sign writer to put up the new company name, and when the lorry pulled up on the forecourt, Mick was surprised to see the name REMICH GARAGES in large letters. He could not help feeling a sense of pride; he was now truly Rene's partner.

The few benches and tools they had were lost in the cavernous building that was their new workplace. There was a lot to be done.

"Rene, we are going to need some desks and files for the offices and more benches and tools for the workshop. We need to contact the petrol suppliers to fill up those tanks on the forecourt and check that the pumps are working. We need to employ staff for the forecourt and at least two more mechanics. We need to contact the telephone company to get the phones connected. We need…"

"Slow down, we must be methodical, let's write a list of all these jobs and then you and I can divide them up and action them, otherwise we'll be running around getting nowhere."

Mick knew that Rene was right, it was just that he was so excited, like a child let loose in a sweet shop.

Giselle arrived at midday with a packed lunch and a bottle of wine and, with Jules, the four stood round one of the benches, which acted as a makeshift table while they ate. Fully sated they returned to the task in hand with Giselle assigned to cleaning the offices. By six o'clock that evening there was the semblance of a business, albeit that there were no vehicles to repair in the workshop, but at least the petrol pumps were working. Jules had learnt how to operate them, having already filled up half a dozen cars after owners had seen that the garage had reopened. It was the start of what would prove to be a very busy week.

It was surprising how quickly word spread around the city that the garage had reopened, and it was being run by an Englishman and his French father-in-law. For some reason this combination intrigued the burgers of Bayeux. Mick was not bothered as to the reason customers came, only that they came!

CHAPTER TWENTY-FIVE

James was due to go back to university in two days and wanted to fit the last piece of the jigsaw together before he went. He had the name of the solicitors who acted for Mr Furford, but was not sure if they would speak to him. After all, he had no real proof that he was his great grandson and they might easily refuse to pass on any information that might be sensitive. There was only one way to find out.

He rang directory enquiries and gave them the name and address of Davies and Renshaw. The phone went quiet while the operator looked for the number, after a while the girl came back on the line with the information.

Tentatively he dialled the number and waited.

"Good morning. Davies and Renshaw, how can I help you?" The young woman's voice was polite and warm and James let out a sigh of relief. That was the first hurdle over, now for the difficult part.

"Hello, I'd like to speak to the person who acted for a Mr Furford of Furford Garage... he er... died about thirty years ago."

"Please hold while I find someone to help you."

The phone went silent. He waited for what seemed an eternity but was probably only a couple of minutes. Then the warm friendly voice came back on the line.

"I'll put you through to Mr Renshaw senior, he said he would be able to help you."

The phone clicked in his ear as the girl transferred him to Mr Renshaw.

"Hello David Renshaw here, how can I help you?"

James had decided to get straight to the point and explain the background only if necessary.

"Hello, thanks for speaking to me. My name is James Harris and I believe Mr Furford was my great grandfather. I am trying to trace what happened to him and his descendants. I understand that you acted for him when his garage burnt down."

"Yes that is correct. I was a junior then, but the case was straightforward and my father, one of the original partners, let me sort it out. I suppose you are aware that Mr Furford died not long after the incident?"

"Yes I had heard, but he had a son who was my mother's father, (he had decided to be bold and assume what he suspected was indeed true) and I wondered if he saw his father after the war?" It was a long shot but he hoped the solicitor might know where Mick was.

"I'm afraid Mr Furford's son has not been heard of, although Mr Furford did leave his estate to his son in the form of a trust fund. Interestingly his instructions were that the principle sum was to be invested and the profits from the investment to be paid annually to St Mary's Hospital. This was in recognition of the treatment they had given his wife who died of pneumonia. The capital sum remains should Mr Furford junior claim it, however, if it is unclaimed after thirty years from the date of the will then the whole sum goes to the hospital. I remember it was the strangest will I ever drew up, but he was convinced his son would come back one day. If you are his great grandson then you surely know what happened to your grandfather."

"That's the problem, I don't."

"I am afraid I don't understand Mr Harris, you don't know?"

James realised that he must sound rather ridiculous, so decided to tell the solicitor the whole story. Mr Renshaw listened in silence as James relayed the events of the last few weeks.

"I see, so you believe that your mother is Mr Michael Furford's daughter, but you do not know if your grandfather is alive or dead, have I got the gist of it?"

"Yes, exactly."

"And does your mother intend to make a claim on the estate? I have to tell you she will need proof of her father's death before we can release the capital."

"No... no... she just wants to find her father... to find the truth."

"Oh I see, my apologies, I am so used to people who are after all they can get, I tend to be a bit of a cynic. Well I can tell you that until you rang no one had even asked about the inheritance. If you leave me your details I will put them on file, and should anyone else make any enquiries, I promise to keep you informed. Though I think after all this time it is highly unlikely, after all there is only six months left to make a claim."

"Thank you, you have been very helpful, I am due back at university the day after tomorrow, so I'll give you my phone number there as well as home."

James dictated the numbers and his home address to the solicitor and, after thanking him again, put the phone down.

Jayne had been sitting patiently in the kitchen and had heard James's side of the conversation, but had not really understood what was going on. She looked enquiringly at him as he walked in from the hall.

"Well?"

"Another inheritance is coming your way!"

"I know that's not true, don't forget I could hear your side of the conversation."

James laughed, he was just winding his mother up, but she was too cute to bite. He relayed the contents of the telephone call to her and waited for a reaction.

"So to sum things up, my father has been left two inheritances but nobody knows if he is dead or alive."

"Succinct but true."

"Thank you James, but was it all worth it? I mean I still never got to meet my father, or in fact prove he was my father. It's all a bit circumstantial, and from what you have learnt, the second inheritance will go to the hospital if it's not claimed by next March."

She couldn't help feeling deflated. At first she had been quietly excited; the locket had awoken something that she had suppressed for years, but it was as if they were back to square one.

CHAPTER TWENTY-SIX

Mick was exhausted but happy. For the last five years he had worked almost round the clock to build up the business. They had not taken a holiday in all that time but there had never been a word of complaint from Giselle. She was part of the 'team' and had taken to the administration like a duck to water. The only person who perhaps was less content was Rene, who found it hard to keep up with the relentless pace set by his son-in-law.

There had of course been some benefits along the way. The family had moved from the village and bought a house in the city, which was larger with four bedrooms, drawing room and a separate dining room. Reluctantly Giselle had agreed to employ a housekeeper, a decision which she only made when Mick gave her the ultimatum of giving up the office, or having a housekeeper.

'Remich' had gained a reputation for quality work at a fair price and there had been no need to advertise, word of mouth had provided an endless stream of customers. Under Mick's tutelage Jules had become a skilled mechanic, and along with the other five that they had employed, the workforce could handle any job large or small. The petrol pump sales provided welcome cash flow and with the general economy growing, there were now more private as well as commercial vehicles on the roads.

Whilst Mick looked after the workshop Rene concentrated on buying parts. The partners had, from the outset, paid cash for all their purchases and in so doing been able to negotiate better prices than some of their competitors, who often ran up high debts. They had actually paid the balance of the original purchase price in six months and not the twelve that had been agreed. Rene had insisted that both he and Mick would only take a wage out of the company and not pay a dividend, but rather build up a healthy balance at the bank. He was, of the two, the more cautious and wanted to be sure, if there was ever a downturn they would be able to weather the storm. The only time they had broken that rule was when they bought the house. Even then, because they had such a large deposit and were well respected by the bank, they had secured a very favourable mortgage, one which was reducing rapidly.

Rene was immensely proud of his son-in-law but knew that he was not totally content. He could see that he wanted more.

"Michael, I have been looking over the last year's accounts. As you know it's our best year ever…"

"I know Rene but I still think we can do better," he interrupted.

"Please let me finish, you are always so impatient." He was not angry; their conversations often went like this. "I have been thinking that now is the time to maybe take the next step."

"The next step?"

"Yes. You know the carpet warehouse next door to our workshop? Well I had a call today to say that they are moving to Caen and the premises are for sale. Do you think it would be a good idea to buy them and extend the repair shop? It would double our capacity."

"How odd, I have been thinking for some time about that building. It is in such a good position sitting on the corner, it has two frontages. However, I must admit I had a different idea for it than you, I…"

"Oh and what have you in mind?" It was Rene's turn to interrupt.

Mick smiled, it was not often that he stole a march on Rene.

"I thought it would make an excellent car showroom. I believe the time is right to enter the car sales market. If we can become a distributor for a major manufacturer, not only will we get the car sales but also the servicing under the guarantee."

Rene was taken aback, he had never considered the possibility of entering the car sales market, nor had he ever thought that Mick would want to. He had always seen him as hands on, not as a fast talking salesman.

"Michael, as you can see I am stunned, do you not want to expand on our proven success? Do you not think it would be a major risk to enter into an area neither of us understands?"

"Of course it is a risk, but I am not saying stop what we are doing, I am saying let us grow the company by building on our existing name for quality and service, with something which goes hand in glove with what we are known for. People will trust us, how many times have you heard stories of ordinary folk feeling they have been cheated by some slick salesman? We can change all that by being honest… It has worked so far."

Rene sat there letting Mick's words sink in. It was true that customers came from miles around because they had heard they would have a quality job and not be overcharged. In spite of his initial doubts, he could not help but be persuaded by the arguments, and he knew if anyone could make it work it was Mick.

"Well first things first, we must speak to the agent and find out how much they want for the premises. I will ring them this afternoon and arrange for us to have a look around. Do you want me to approach the car manufacturers?" He looked at Mick expectantly, after all he had always been the one negotiating the deals, but he had a feeling that this time it would be different.

"If you have no objection I would like to take the lead on this one."

Mick had confirmed Rene's thoughts, maybe the young lion was about to assume command of the pack!

As always the pair wasted no time in putting their plans into operation. Rene had an appointment to view the old carpet warehouse set up for the next morning, and Mick had three different appointments with manufacturers arranged over the coming two weeks. There was a new buzz of excitement about the place. The entire workforce soon learnt about the plans to expand, and were as keen as Rene and Mick. The partners had fostered a feeling amongst the staff of being part of their extended family, and this had engendered a loyalty which was rare in similar businesses.

They had visited the building next door and as Mick had thought, it was ideal for a car showroom. It would take only minor alterations to the frontage to enable double doors to be fitted, allowing cars in and out. There was only a small paved area at the front so they would be unable to have cars outside, but that was a small price to pay for the advantage of it being attached to their existing property.

After talking it over with Mick, Rene had made an offer to the vendor, which to his delight had been accepted immediately, and once the contracts had been signed he had instructed the builders to commence the alterations. Meanwhile, Mick had already visited the Peugeot factory and was due to visit Renault and Citroen by the end of the next week.

Within a month the showroom was ready, but still Mick had no deal with any of the car manufacturers he had visited. He was beginning to worry, for the first time a doubt in his own ability was creeping in. Rene had no doubts, he believed totally in Mick and felt that his son-in-law was just being impatient. The problem was that all the manufacturers had franchises with large distributors and did not want to upset any of them.

Mick had got on well with the Director at Citroen when they had met, but like the others he was doubtful about taking on a new distributor, especially one with no track record. In a last effort to convince him Mick rang and asked for another meeting; after some persuasion and a lot of pleading, Monsieur Chabal agreed to see him.

Mick pulled up outside the Citroen offices and looked at his watch, it was ten minutes to twelve and his appointment was for twelve o'clock, he hated being late, considering it bad manners.

The young lady at reception took his name and asked him to take a chair, whilst she informed Monsieur Chabal that he was there to see him.

"Monsieur Chabal will be with you in a few minutes," she said from behind her typewriter.

It was not long before a woman of about twenty, slim, with a neat pencil skirt and white blouse, appeared from the lift.

"Monsieur Furford?" She walked across the foyer towards his chair. "Monsieur Chabal will see you now, please follow me."

It was the same girl he had met last time, Chabal's secretary, but she showed no sign of recognition and said nothing as they entered the lift. At the second floor the lift came to a jarring halt and she opened the doors, beckoning him to follow. They walked down a long narrow corridor, at the end of which was a door with a name plate bearing the inscription 'J CHABAL'. She knocked once and entered, Mick following closely behind.

"Good morning Monsieur Furford, how are you?"

Chabal spoke with a slightly nasal accent, which sounded as though he had a permanent cold. He was a tall man, probably six foot three and well built, his very shape gave an aura of authority. Mick had thought the first time they met that this was a man who usually got his own way and was not easily persuaded. The thought re-entered his head and he wondered if this meeting was such a good idea, but it was too late now he was in the lion's den!

"Good morning, I am well thank you."

Mick could feel his hands sweating and his stomach churning.

"From our telephone conversation I understand you have a proposal to put to me?" He looked at Mick quizzically. "Well I'm all ears."

"As I explained last time we met, our company has up to now specialised in repairs and maintenance of cars, small vans and farm machinery and now we feel it is the right time to branch out into car sales."

"Yes. Yes. You explained all that before but what are you proposing? I'm a very busy man and have many other appointments, I would be grateful if you could come to the point."

Things were not going as Mick had planned and his stomach was now doing somersaults.

"My apologies. Our reputation has been built on the quality and value of the service we offer, we have many testimonials to endorse what I am saying. I believe that it is not enough just to sell a quality car like the Citroen, but you must back it up with quality after sales servicing. I would like the opportunity to prove to you that we can give that service. I would ask you to send some of your cars to 'REMICH' and we will service them over a period of one month free of charge. If after that time you are satisfied with the quality and speed of the work, then I would ask that you grant us a franchise, but if you are not happy with even one car that we repair, then we loose the chance of selling your cars."

"You are very sure of yourself, Monsieur Furford, and that is a quality I admire. I accept your offer and agree your terms, but I warn you, our in-house mechanics will monitor you every step of the way and they are very thorough. Let us see just how good you are, the first cars will be delivered tomorrow."

He stood up and walked round the table holding out his hand. Mick took it and they shook hands to seal the agreement.

Mick was still in a daze as he walked to his car, it had been a long shot and at one stage he had wondered if it was a waste of time, but now there was a chance and it was a chance that he would not let slip through his grasp.

As he pulled up outside his house he was still pinching himself in disbelief. Parking the car he bounded up the steps to the door and rushed in straight to the kitchen, where he knew Giselle would be after her day at the office.

"Darling. Darling. I've done it."

She appeared from inside the pantry.

"Done what?"

"Is Rene home?"

"No not yet, done what?"

"I've got the franchise to sell Citroen cars," he exclaimed.

"Fantastic, we must open some champagne, we have a double celebration."

She smiled and he looked puzzled.

"What else are we celebrating then?"

"I'm pregnant!"

"Oh my God."

"That wasn't quite the reaction I wanted," she laughed.

"I'm sorry, it's just I'm so shocked, it's fantastic."

"You'd better sit down, there's more, I'm expecting twins."

"Bloody hell, this is too much in one day."

They were both laughing now. They were still laughing and drinking champagne when Rene came home.

"What on earth is going on, are you two drunk?"

"Yes Papa, drunk with happiness. Tell him Michael."

"Rene, sit down and join us in a glass of champagne, you're going to be a grandfather and not just once but twice, Giselle is expecting twins."

Rene sat down with a thud; he was as shocked as Mick had been at the news.

"I thought you were celebrating something else. So tell me Michael how did your meeting go today?"

"Very well, we will have the franchise in a month's time."

Rene looked at him quizzically.

"Why not now?"

"I have made a deal with him to prove that we are capable and deserve the franchise, it was the only way."

Mick explained the offer he had made to Chabal and that they had shaken hands on it.

"And you believe he will stand by his word?"

"I am sure of it."

There was no more to be said.

For the next month Mick was at the workshop an hour before the normal start and stayed an hour later at night. He checked and double checked every car that was sent over from the Citroen factory, nothing left the premises without his personal approval.

The last Citroen car left the workshop four weeks from the date of his meeting. It had been a long hard slog, but they had managed to complete the extra work and not let a single customer down. Mick felt mentally and physically exhausted and now he must wait to see if they had been successful. The next day he had no breakfast, lunch or dinner, he could not face any food, his stomach knotted with anxiety. The following day came and went and still he could not eat. Giselle was worried, he looked tired and grey.

On the third day the office phone rang and the receptionist called Mick, over the Tannoy, to come to the phone.

"Michael, I have a Monsieur Chabal on the line for you," she said as he came through the door from the workshop.

"Good morning, Michael Furford speaking." His voice trembled as he spoke.

"Mr Furford, when we last met we made a deal. You have kept your side of the bargain and now I am keeping mine. Can you call in at the factory on Monday to sign the paperwork? I am pleased to offer you a franchise to sell Citroen cars and might I say, if you are as successful at selling as you are at repairs, then we will have long and profitable relationship."

"Thank you, thank you. Yes I will be with you on Monday. Thank you." The relief in his voice was audible.

CHAPTER TWENTY-SEVEN

Jayne was slowly getting back into the routine of a new term. She had spent the last couple of days of the summer break catching up on her notes and preparing the lessons. The start of a new term was always hectic and, along with her colleagues, she had been back at school before the term started properly, ironing out any changes to the curriculum and checking timetables. It was all so familiar that she could almost do it in her sleep, but as soon as the doors opened to let the children in, that old buzz came back. If there was one thing she loved more than anything, except James and Nigel of course, it was teaching.

At lunchtime she found a quiet corner in the staff room and sat down to catch up on the newspapers and eat her Ryvita and spread. Each new term she would start a diet, but it usually lasted only a few days before a reason came along for its abandonment.

Janet, who taught History and who had become her closest friend at school, walked in and crossed the room to join her.

"So how was your holiday? Go anywhere nice?" she asked Jayne

"I didn't go anywhere actually. It was Nigel's last break before starting university and James was home, so I just wanted to spend time with them, though Nigel has a new girlfriend so I didn't see all that much of him." She smiled to herself at the thought of Nigel and Clare and the shock when she had first met Clare.

"Oh. Rather boring then. I must tell you about my holiday. You remember last term I told you I had met this French guy who was teaching in that new comprehensive school?"

Jayne nodded knowing not to interrupt her when she was in full flow.

"Well he invited me to visit his family in Grasse, that's near Nice you know," she said rather patronisingly.

Jayne ignored the remark.

"As I was saying, he invited me over and we stayed there for four weeks, it was fantastic... and so was he. Christ can that man make love!"

"Janet, keep your voice down everyone's looking." Jayne felt embarrassed, though why she didn't know.

Not wanting to be outdone by Janet's revelations, Jayne could not resist telling her about the locket and all that James had found out regarding her father.

"Crikey! So you're related to the aristocracy then?"

"Not exactly and anyway, I can't prove it because my father's name was not on my birth certificate."

"But surely the picture in the locket and everything else is enough proof?"

"Not in a court of law and with a serious amount of money at stake, then I'm sure someone would contest it."

Nothing more was said on the subject as the bell rang to signal the start of the first period after lunch.

That evening, curled up on the sofa with a mug of coffee, Jayne reflected on her conversation with Janet earlier.

It was not the inheritance that bothered her, although truth to tell the money would be very useful, it was the fact that her long-suppressed interest in her father had now come to prominence.

As she sat there thinking about her father, her mind went back over the years to the men who had been surrogate fathers during her life.

She had been six years old when her mother married Harold Davies and, as she had never had a father before, did not take easily to him, but then he had never made much of an effort with her. He was that much older than her mother, nearly as old as her grandmother, and lacked the energy and inclination to be bothered with a small child. He was kind and never ever, as far as she could remember, had he shouted at her. In fact, for the short time that he was part of the family, before his untimely death, he had not made much of an impression on her.

Her mother's second husband, on the other hand, did leave a lasting memory.

CHAPTER TWENTY-EIGHT

After the death of Harold Davies, Jayne, her mother and grandma settled down to a quiet routine of domesticity that did not include menfolk, but it was not to last long. Isabel had always been susceptible to flattery and a manager in the tool room at the factory had taken her eye. Grandma Brown was not aware at first that her daughter was anything but settled in her life as a spinster, after all she had settled for it, so why shouldn't Isabel.

Harvey was the opposite of Harold Davies; he was about five eleven with sandy hair and clean shaven. At thirty-eight he was one of the younger managers who had worked their way up from the shop floor, and his hands were gnarled from the work he had done as a younger man. He had not been called up for the forces as the factory had been turned over to munitions during the fighting, and he had been deemed too important to leave his job. Although he had rather a sallow complexion, he had sparkling blue eyes and it was this that attracted the women. Isabel had not been the only female at the company that found him charming and, although he had somewhat of a reputation as a ladies' man, she had not been deterred.

Isabel not only found him attractive, but was pleased to discover that he was single. Although he had been married once, it was when he was much younger and it had not lasted very long. His wife had left him and they had quickly divorced. There had been no children. It was strange, but if Isabel brought up the subject of his wife and asked why they had split up he always changed the subject, saying that it had been a painful experience and one that he preferred not to talk about. After a few times of asking she decided to forget it, after all it was in the past and it was the future that she was interested in now.

It was seven months before Isabel took the plunge and introduced Harvey to her mother. She had gone out for a drink as she usually did on a Friday night and her mother was looking after Jayne.

Mrs Brown heard the key turning in the front door and instinctively looked up at the clock on the mantelpiece, strange it was only nine thirty and Isabel did not usually get home until about eleven.

"Is that you Isabel?" she called from the living room.

"Yes Mum, I've got someone with me I'd like you to meet."

Mrs Brown stood up, brushing imaginary creases from her skirt as she did so. Who on earth had Isabel brought in at this time of night? It was obviously not Grace; she would have just walked in without introduction.

It came as shock when Isabel walked into the living room with a young man following her.

"Mum this is Harvey, Harvey Jameson, he works at the factory with me."

Harvey held his hand out to Mrs Brown, who tentatively took it and gave a cursory shake.

"Pleased to meet you Mrs Brown, Isabel has told me so much about you." He gave a thin smile.

Isabel's mother was always quick to form opinions of people and did so now; there was something about this man that she took an instant dislike to!

"How do you do Mr Jameson?"

"Please, call me Harvey." The thin smile appeared again.

"Mum I wanted you to meet Harvey because we have been seeing each other for a few weeks now, and I want to introduce him to Jayne, but I'd like you to sort of prepare the ground for me."

"I see, well that depends on how serious things are between you two. I don't think you need say anything to Jayne at this stage, not until you decide your future intentions."

Isabel could see things were not going as she had planned so decided not to labour the point.

Harvey also detected the frosty atmosphere and decided a dignified withdrawal was the best strategy.

"Well, I best be getting off home then, goodnight Mrs Brown, a pleasure to meet you." He did not wait for a reply and made his way to the door.

Isabel followed him.

"Don't worry she'll come round, she doesn't like change, she'll be fine."

"I hope so Isabel, you know I really love you don't you?"

"Yes of course I do." She put her arms round his neck and kissed him hard on the mouth. "It will be okay." She was trying to reassure herself as much as him.

She closed the door and went back into the living room.

"You were a bit off with Harvey, you might as well know he has asked me to marry him and I've said yes."

"I just hope you know what you're doing that's all."

Nothing more was said on the subject that night and it was another two weeks before Isabel brought Harvey home again, but this time it was to meet Jayne.

Isabel was not one to let the grass grow under her feet and was soon sporting an engagement ring which she showed to everyone she met, whether she knew them or not!

The wedding took place on December 1st 1950; Jayne was nine and half and excited about being her mother's only bridesmaid, though could not understand why she was not allowed to go on the honeymoon with her mother and new daddy. After all, they had said it was a holiday and she always had holidays with her mother.

Jayne stayed with her grandmother who, whilst accepting her new son-in-law, did not take him to her bosom. Mrs Brown did not fall for his easy charm the way that the younger women seemed to, but she held her council and decided that for her daughter's sake she must at least try and like him.

On returning from the honeymoon Harvey moved his personal belongings into the house on the Tamworth Road. He had lived with his parents in a small terraced house in the Stoke area, so the move was a step up the ladder in his eyes.

To Jayne, who was not used to men being around, it was difficult to adjust. Before, she had always had immediate access to both her mother and her grandma, but now Harvey came first, at least with her mother. Jayne inevitably grew closer to her grandma.

It appeared at times as though the house was divided in two: Harvey and Isabel in one part and Jayne and her grandmother in the other. Isabel didn't seem to mind as it meant that she and her new husband could go out almost whenever they wanted, as grandma was only too happy to be the 'baby sitter'.

With each passing month Isabel and her mother seemed to grow more distant from each other, whilst not actually falling out. Whenever Harvey came in, Grandma Brown would withdraw to another room and often Jayne would join her.

Harvey accepted the situation and in fact was secretly pleased; he had never had children of his own and did not want any. He and Isabel had discussed the subject before they were married and had both agreed that they would not start a family; he was not unkind to Jayne, just not interested.

Jayne passed her eleven plus examination and got a place at the grammar school; it was at that point that she decided that she wanted to be a teacher. She soon settled in at her new school, was good at sports and popular amongst her peers. Her reports for her first year were glowing, but although her teachers were quick to praise her, she retained her popularity with her classmates and was never accused of being a swot or teachers pet.

Her mother was pleased with her attitude and even Harvey had been impressed, though not being academic himself had been of little help with her homework. For some reason that she could not explain she had never got close to Harvey, but then he had never tried to get close to her. They lived in the same house but her mother was oblivious to their relationship.

Over the next five years life at home was uneventful. Her mother had her career; her stepfather was kind to her without interfering and she was the apple of her grandmother's eye. To Mrs Brown she could do no wrong, and on the odd occasion when she did step out of line, it was Isabel that meted out the punishment and grandma that offered the consoling shoulder to cry on. If Isabel felt unsupported by her mother she certainly got no help from Harvey, whose standard line was…

"She's your daughter not mine."

Fortunately these incidents were few and far between so any tension was soon dissipated.

Jayne was coming up to her sixteenth birthday and she was due to sit her 'O' levels in the June. The minimum requirement for a university place was three 'A' passes and Jayne was quietly confident of achieving that, having already applied to three different universities for a place. Her plans were rudely interrupted by the events that were about to unfold.

She would never forget that night. It was Friday and as usual Harvey went for a drink straight after work, this particular Friday was different. It was eight o'clock and his dinner had been ready for an hour, but still no sign of Harvey. Isabel was getting worried but was reluctant to call the Red Lion in case it annoyed him. When ten thirty, closing time, came and he still hadn't arrived, panic set in. Isabel phoned the pub but the landlord had not seen him at all that night. Now she really began to worry, her mind imaging all sorts of explanations including a fatal accident. Grandma Brown tried to calm her down but to no avail. Jayne did not go to bed but stayed up to comfort her mother.

At eleven o'clock she could wait no longer and rang the police to report him missing. After giving a description of Harvey, she then had to wait while the constable noted everything down and then spoke to his sergeant. It felt like an eternity before he came back on the line with the fateful words.

"Your husband is under arrest and is helping us with our enquires."

Isabel almost dropped the phone in shock.

"Under arrest, what for?" she asked.

"I'm afraid I can't say anything at this time, I suggest you speak to Inspector Donaldson. I will get him to ring you when he is free."

Jayne had tried to comfort her mother but she was too agitated and insisted on going to the police station straight away.

She did not return for three hours and Jayne and her grandmother were still up when she finally came home.

"Harvey's been arrested and charged with theft." The words spilled from her mouth between bursts of tears.

"Isabel, calm down and explain exactly what's going on." Mrs Brown had put her arm around her daughter to comfort her, whist Jayne had made a cup of tea for the three of them.

"He's been arrested as part of a gang who have been stealing engine parts, apparently it's been going on over a period of years, and selling them to local garages and to anyone else who would pay cash. He was not working alone but is accused of being the ringleader. I can't believe it. If it's true where is the money he is supposed to have received? I certainly haven't seen any of it."

"So what happens now? Are they going to release him?" Her mother was ever the practical one.

"No that's the worse part, they won't give him bail for fear he will abscond. I've got to get him a solicitor and with it being Saturday tomorrow, it means he will be held until Monday at the earliest."

"I think we all need to get to bed, I'm sure things will look better in the morning." Mrs Brown was convinced she was right, but the morning would bring no relief to Isabel.

The first thing Isabel did on the Monday was to phone her office and explain that she needed a couple of days off to sort out some personal matters. She did not have to explain what those 'personal matters' were, as the news had spread around the factory like wildfire. Her next call was to the solicitor to ask him to go to the police station to see if he could get Harvey bail. In spite of all his efforts, Harvey was not granted bail and was formally charged to appear at the Magistrates' Court the following week.

When Isabel went to the court she was astonished to hear how serious the case was, and all the defendants were remanded to appear at the Crown Court in six weeks' time. She had visited Harvey in prison and he had told her that it was untrue, that the police had got him confused with someone else, that he was totally innocent and would sue the police for hundreds of pounds.

On returning home from her visit her mother asked what had transpired.

"Mum, to tell you the truth I don't know where I am. I still can't believe Harvey's done this. After all it's not as if there is any money about the house, and even the police have checked both our bank accounts and found nothing. So if he's this mastermind of a criminal, where are the spoils?"

Mrs Brown wisely kept her council. She had never taken to Harvey right from the first day they met, and she was quite sure he was capable of anything.

When the case finally came to trial, it was alleged that Harvey was a compulsive gambler and a poor one to boot, who needed money to feed his addiction. He was said to have stolen to pay off massive debts. Isabel was shocked because she had no idea of his problem. At home he had covered his tracks, if not at work!

Harvey was found guilty and sentenced to four years. Isabel had filed for divorce within weeks of the sentence. She had been betrayed and no amount of contrition on Harvey's part would change her mind. Jayne and her grandmother had not been sorry to see the back of Harvey, but Grandma Brown wisely never said 'I told you so'.

The three women, for Jayne was now maturing into a well developed young lady, settled back into their old lives.

Jayne had managed to stay focused during the upheaval and had duly passed her 'A' levels, winning a place at university.

Isabel felt sad but extremely proud when Jayne started university, the house was suddenly quieter without her daughter and ex-husband.

CHAPTER TWENTY-NINE

Ron Harris had been Jayne's boyfriend from the age of fifteen; they had met at a school dance. He was a pupil at the boys' grammar school, which was paired with her all girls' school and each year at Christmas they held a joint dance.

Ron was not a shy boy and had made a beeline for Jayne the minute the dancing started; none of his friends had a look in. Jayne was flattered and despite many of her friends telling her not to get too serious, she was hooked. They were childhood sweethearts from that moment onwards.

Ron was not as academic as Jayne and, although he passed five 'O' levels, decided to leave school when he was sixteen and get a job. He had set his heart on being a salesman and took a job in a small factory making machine parts, so that he could learn all about the products. He was hoping to impress his boss into letting him join the sales team. The one thing that he had going for him was his personality, he had the knack of being able to talk to complete strangers and hold a conversation on almost any subject. The one thing he did not lack was confidence.

He had been with the company for eighteen months and had done every job in the factory, so impressing his boss with his tenacity that he been offered a trial as a salesman. Meanwhile Jayne had sat her 'A' levels and obtained her place at university; Isabel had wondered how the relationship would survive with them being apart, and was quite shocked when Jayne said that they were getting engaged. She had been convinced that after a few weeks on his own he would be like most men, and move on to pastures new.

At the end of the first year, Jayne had arrived home full of news about her new friends, and how well the course was going. Her big news that she wanted to tell her mother and grandma was that she and Ron were definitely getting married, as soon as she finished her university course in two more years.

So it was a shock to find that Grandma Brown was not there to greet her. It was an even bigger shock when Isabel told her, that her grandmother had cancer and had only three months to live. Jayne had burst into tears and wanted to go to the hospital immediately.

"Does she know?" Jayne asked her mother.

"Yes," she said flatly.

"But when? How long have you known?"

"She was diagnosed two months ago. She's had chemotherapy but it hasn't worked."

"Why didn't you tell me, I could have come home?"

"Grandma didn't want you bothered, it was her decision."

The tears reappeared and Isabel comforted her daughter.

"I know, I know. You must be strong. It's what she would want."

Mother and daughter held each other, each drawing strength from the other, not wanting to break the embrace, hoping that it was just a bad dream. Like many other families the killer had struck, showing them no mercy or compassion.

Jayne visited her grandmother that night and found it difficult not to cry when she saw her. Grandma Brown had not been a big woman, but was now so thin that she looked like the pictures Jayne had seen of prisoners of war. She stayed for some time talking about university, her friends, in fact anything that came into her head, anything that is except the 'C' word. The nurse came at 8.00 o'clock to say that all visitors must leave and as she said her goodbyes, on an impulse, Jayne turned to her grandmother.

"I almost forgot the big news, Ron and I are getting married before I go back to uni."

"Really! Are you sure you're ready for this, it's a big step you know? Don't you think you should wait until you have finished your course?"

"No, no we've talked it through and worked out that if Ron lives with his parents for the next two years and saves hard, then we can afford a deposit on a house. When I come home for holidays he can come to our house so we can be together. Don't worry, we have it all worked out." She bent down and kissed the old lady, turned and left without another word.

Once outside of the hospital Jayne panicked. What if Ron wouldn't get married straight away? She had dived in and her mouth had run away with her, but she wanted so much for her grandmother to see her getting married and they hadn't got much time.

Fortunately, Ron was all for it. There was no doubt that he was in love with Jayne, but the relationship had never got past the heavy petting stage and, considering that they were engaged, he was getting distinctively frustrated!

Isabel did not pass comment; she was hardly in a position to question her daughter, though she did think that they were a little young. Isabel understood Jayne's reasons and respected her wishes; she knew that her mother had always wanted to be at Jayne's wedding, she just hoped the hospital would let her come out to be there.

The marriage took place on the 28th of July, the day of her nineteenth birthday. Grandma Brown had been determined that she would be there, and the hospital had pumped her full of drugs to see her through the day, but by seven that evening she was struggling and they called for a taxi to take her back to the ward. As soon as her head hit the pillow she was asleep. She never woke up.

Jayne and Ron had left for their honeymoon in Cornwall and therefore did not hear the news until they returned a week later. Although Jayne was sad, at least her grandma's dying wish had been fulfilled.

Isabel had never given up her job even though in the past Harvey had suggested she should, and now she was glad that she kept it. It gave her a certain independence, and with her mother gone and Jayne at university, she needed something to occupy her mind. Jayne and Ron stayed with Isabel whenever she was home from university, an arrangement that worked well enough, but it meant that Isabel was alone during term time.

When Jayne finally finished her course, she and Ron moved into a small terraced house on a new estate on the east side of the city.

Isabel was on her own now and, after living so long with company in the house, found it difficult to fully adjust, though it was to prove a short-lived loneliness.

CHAPTER THIRTY

Jayne and Ron had bought their house through a local estate agent, Hastings and Co. They dealt with the proprietor a Mr Granville Hastings, who had been more than helpful in that he had also arranged their mortgage for them.

Isabel had accompanied her daughter on a number of occasions when she visited the agents or went to view the new house. It was Jayne that first noticed that Mr Grenville seemed to be taking an interest in Isabel.

"You know Mum, Mr Hastings seems to spend more time telling you about the house rather than me. I think he fancies you." She was teasing her mother but nevertheless she was sure it was true.

"Don't be silly. You're imagining things." Isabel blushed slightly at the thought.

Her embarrassment was even greater the following week when the local florists drew up outside her house with a beautiful bouquet of flowers with a note saying: 'Beautiful flowers for a beautiful lady'.

Isabel could not deny that she was flattered and phoned to thank him. This was the opportunity that he had been hoping for, and he wasted no time in asking to take her out for a meal that weekend.

Granville was forty-five years old and a confirmed bachelor, that was until he met Isabel and was totally smitten. After that first date he bombarded her with flowers and was always 'in the area' at weekends, so that he could pop in and see her. He was a handsome man, about five foot nine with brown hair and a ginger beard and had a slight build. His only fault appeared to be a chronic case of verbal diarrhoea... he knew everything about everything! Five minutes in his company and people would start to switch off. For some reason Isabel didn't notice this trait and was flattered by his attention; it had been a long time since a man had shown this much interest, without wanting to get her into bed after one dinner date.

The courting lasted four or five months before he finally plucked up the courage to ask her to marry him, a request she accepted with alacrity. The wedding date was set for the following August, a day that was to prove memorable for the fact that it rained constantly all day. Luckily they were honeymooning in Tuscany and spent the next two weeks in a mini heat wave.

After the honeymoon Isabel moved into Granville's house, which was a large five-bedroom property on the Kenilworth Road, with its own drive and trees hiding it from the busy road outside. Isabel wanted to put her own house on the market but Grenville had other ideas. He suggested that as Jayne was her only daughter and they were not planning to have any children, why not present her with the Tamworth Road house? Isabel could not grasp exactly what he was suggesting at first and it took a while before the penny dropped.

"Granville are you serious? That house is worth a considerable sum and I thought I would sell it and buy into your house." Isabel had thought this was the only fair thing to do.

"Darling, you know I'm not short of a bob or two and as far as I'm concerned, we're a couple now. What's mine is yours and all that."

"But Granville that is so generous, you really are something special." She reached up and kissed him gently on the lips.

"As long as you are happy, then so am I." He gave her a squeeze as if to seal the plan.

When Isabel told her, Jayne was flabbergasted, she had not realised just how kind Granville was and felt a little guilty about describing him to her friends as 'a bit of a bore'.

Isabel had accepted Granville's offer on one condition, that for the next ten years the house would be in Jayne's name alone. Deep down she was worried that a marriage between two very young people might not last, after ten years then Jayne could do what she wanted and have the house in joint names if she preferred.

Isabel was not to know at the time just how prophetic she had been.

When Jayne told Ron of her mother's gift he was only too pleased to accept, and did not give the 'ten year condition' a second thought. They were able to sell their new house at a profit and bank a clear five thousand pounds, plus no more mortgage repayments. It was like winning the football pools.

Of all her step-fathers, Granville was the one that Jayne had the least to do with. She was married herself and although she saw her mother often, Granville would either be working, weekends being a busy time for him, or he would be reading in his study. She still found him a bit boring and when they did get together as a family, she would engineer things so that someone else got lumbered with him. However, she always felt slightly ashamed of herself for doing this. In fairness to Granville, she could not deny that over the years he had always been kind to her mother and thought the world of her.

Jayne had been sitting reflecting on the three men who had been her stepfathers and in retrospect felt the best had been Granville. The empty coffee cup sat on the table next to her and looking up she noticed that it was ten o'clock. She must have sat there for the best part of two hours.

"I wonder if I will ever meet my real father?" The question hung in the air, addressed to no one in particular for there was no one who could answer it.

CHAPTER THIRTY-ONE

The birth of the twins was probably the most traumatic event of Mick's life, at least as far as he could remember. He was busy at work when the call came through from Giselle.

"Michael, I need you quickly, I've started, we must get to the hospital." The words poured out in a torrent. He could tell that she was frightened at the prospect of the birth.

"Darling, take it easy, don't panic, I'll be with you in ten minutes. Just take it easy, everything will be fine." His voice was reassuring but inside he felt as nervous as she sounded.

He quickly washed his hands, changed out of his overalls and jumped into his car. Even though the company was expanding he still spent most of his day in the workshops, although more in a supervisory role. It was important to him that the standards they had set from the start were maintained.

The car screeched to a standstill in the drive and without bothering to close the door after him he ran up the steps to their door. His hand was shaking and the key would not engage properly in the lock. After a few choice words he finally got the door open and called out for Giselle.

"I'm in the kitchen, the suitcase is packed ready in the bedroom, can you fetch it?"

Without replying he went upstairs, taking the treads two at a time.

"Right let's get you to hospital." He kissed her on the cheek and squeezed her hand as if to say everything is okay.

They reached the hospital in no time at all and were checked in by a nurse, who had obviously seen it all before, because there was no way she was going to be hurried. By the time Giselle was safely ensconced on the ward the contractions had stopped!

The doctor came to see them after about half an hour and examined her.

"There is no problem, soon the contractions will begin again and then we will re-examine you, but for now just relax."

Mick sat next to his wife holding her hand and occasionally squeezing it. He looked at her... she was beautiful.

Two hours had elapsed and the contractions were now repeating at an ever increasing rate. Mick was not sure what to do, should he stay with Giselle or go and look for a nurse? When they hadn't needed one there seemed to be plenty of nurses but now there were none.

Giselle let out yet another moan and her face contorted with the pain. Mick decided he must do something and letting go of her hand walked quickly down the corridor, wanting to run but managing to control the urge. He was nearly at the hospital entrance before he finally spotted a young nurse.

"Excuse me, my wife is in labour and I think the babies are coming."

"Don't worry I'll fetch the midwife, please go back to your wife, we'll be with you in a couple of minutes."

Mick returned to the ward where Giselle was now crying with the pain. He felt quite useless, unable to either offer relief or even share the agony she was enduring.

"Please, Mr Furford, would you please go to the waiting room. Your wife is in good hands and it looks as though the babies are on the way." The midwife's tone was kindly but firm.

With a last squeeze of her hand he got up from the chair beside her bed and slowly, almost reluctantly, walked along the corridor to the waiting room.

He tried to read one of the magazines that lay on the table but could not concentrate, his nerves jangling, the waiting almost claustrophobic.

Fortunately he did not have to wait long, within an hour the same nurse that he had found in the corridor poked her head around the door.

"Mr Furford, please follow me, your wife has two beautiful boys."

A smile spread across his face as the news slowly sank in. Although they knew they were expecting twins they had not speculated on what sex they might be.

Giselle was sitting up in the bed a small bundle in each arm.

"You wonderful, clever, brilliant girl." The words gushed out making her smile, a smile of pride and love.

"Michael come closer. Do you want to hold one?"

"No I want to hold them both." He laughed; the tension of the last few hours now completely disappeared.

Giselle laughed with him. It was typical of him, making light of a situation, it was his 'trademark'.

They spent the next hour soaking in the sheer pleasure of holding their new family, and the unsaid self-congratulatory feeling they were both experiencing.

Mick broke the spell.

"I must tell Rene, he will be worried."

He kissed Giselle and told her to get some rest whilst he went back to the office with the good news. He knew that Rene would want to visit his daughter and grandchildren as soon as he heard.

At the garage they did not need to ask if everything was well, the stupid grin on his face was all the information they needed, but he would not speak to anyone until he had told Rene.

Rene's office door was open before he had chance to knock.

"How is she? Is everything okay? How are the babies? Can I see her?" The barrage of questions hit Mick as he walked up to his father-in-law.

"Slow down." The grin was even wider now. "She's fine and so are the boys."

"Boys?" Rene's eyes showed surprise.

"Yes, boys and they are healthy, crying like all babies. Would you like to go and see them?" Mick knew it was a rhetorical question, there would be no way of stopping him.

At the hospital Rene kissed his daughter, tears running down his eyes.

"If only your mother could have been here."

Giselle could not help crying at this remark and even Mick had a lump in his throat, but the joy of the moment quickly replaced the sadness.

"What are you going to call them?" Rene asked.

It was something that neither Giselle nor Mick had thought about that morning. They had in the past few weeks discussed numerous names for both boys and girls, but had not actually picked any as special favourites.

"Papa, would you mind waiting outside for a few minutes? There is something I need to discuss with Michael."

Rene looked up, a little put out by the request but Giselle smiled at him and he had never been able to resist that smile. As he left the room Mick looked quizzically at his wife, what on earth did she want to say that could not be said in front of Rene?

"Darling, I don't think you know this but papa has three other names beside Rene. His full name is Rene, Peter, Oliver, Charles; would you consider calling the boys Peter and Oliver?"

"I think it's a fantastic idea and I think Rene would be very proud, the only problem is he will probably burst into tears again when we tell him."

They both laughed because they knew that there was no doubt on that score.

Mick walked down to the waiting room to collect Rene and brought him back into the ward.

"Rene," Mick said in a very formal fashion. "We have reached a very important decision."

Rene's brow furrowed and he looked worried, what was this decision and why was Mick so serious.

"Rene, we have…." Mick burst out laughing. "It's no good I can't keep this up. The truth is we have decided to name the boys Peter and Oliver after their favourite grandfather."

As predicted Rene burst into tears, but they were proud, joyful tears.

CHAPTER THIRTY-TWO

The twins had not been identical when they were born, and now that they were five years old not only did they look different, but were developing their own personalities. Peter was the eldest, by four minutes and he was showing signs of his seniority. If there was an argument or squabble over toys then Peter usually got his way. He was definitely the more outgoing of the two and would happily go to any stranger, where Oliver hid behind his mother's skirts until the newcomer gently won him round.

They were similar in height and obviously brothers, having the same dark curly hair inherited from their mother, but Peter was the heavier of the two and had been the first to walk, though strangely it was Oliver who had been the first to talk. Mick and Giselle had spoken to them in both French and English from day one, so they were bi-lingual, a feat that amazed Rene who had never been able to master English despite all of Mick's help.

"You know it's strange that the boys are so different." Mick had just put them to bed and was sitting opposite Giselle in the kitchen. "Peter is so full of himself whilst Oliver is far more serious, even at this age they have very diverse characters."

"Well I like the fact that they look and act differently. I have never thought it healthy to dress two children the same and have folk not being able to tell them apart."

"I agree, I was just wondering how they will turn out when they are older."

"There's plenty of time to find that out, they have only just started school, do you want them at the factory already?" Giselle tut tutted as she spoke, but in his head it was exactly what he was planning.

Rene had overheard the conversation and smiled. He knew how ambitious Mick was, and had thought from the first day that if boys were born, Mick would want them to be part of the 'dynasty'.

"Michael, excuse me for interrupting your conversation with your wife but can I have a word?"

Mick turned to his father-in-law.

"Of course, is it about the boys?"

"No, far more boring, it is about work."

"Rene is there something wrong?"

"No, no it's just that in the last few years we have opened up a new garage each year: St Lo, Coutances, Valognee and Cherbourg." Mick was about to interrupt, but he held up his hand. "Let me continue. I have been behind you and supported you each time and I have to confess you have made it work. I had my doubts about Cherbourg; I thought you had overstretched us but yet again it was a winner. You have worked hard and made us very wealthy in the process. We don't owe anyone a single franc, everything is paid for, but my friend, when is it going to end? Can we not rest on our laurels and enjoy our success?"

Mick sat there listening to what Rene had said, he knew it was true that he had pushed and pushed but he still had a dream.

"Rene, I will confess to you that from the very first day that we obtained the franchise to sell Citroens, I wanted to have a garage and showroom in Caen, but it was impossible because Duval Motors had the franchise for the area."

"And now it is possible, am I right?"

Mick was taken aback, he had said nothing until he was himself sure of the facts.

"What do you mean?"

"Michael I am your partner, do you keep secrets from me?"

Mick went a deep shade of red. He had never had a secret from Rene, but this was different and he had wanted to marshal all of his facts before presenting the case to Rene.

"Rene, I apologise, I have behaved very badly I should have spoken to you sooner, my only excuse was that I wanted all the facts to present to you before we discussed it, but I see that was wrong, can you forgive me?"

"Michael, you are like a son to me, of course I forgive you, but please never put me in that position again. I only knew something was going on because I took a phone call from Jacque

Duvall, who was calling you, but you were out visiting St Lo. I said I would get you to call him back tomorrow. Now will you please let me in on your little secret?" He smiled as he finished speaking to let Mick know that he was not annoyed with him.

Mick looked embarrassed and guilty.

"I had a call from Chabal at the Citroen plant last Thursday to tell me that Duval was considering retiring, putting his company up for sale and would I be interested. I should have said something then, but I wanted to check with Duval that the information was correct. I phoned him, he said that he had mentioned to Chabal that he was thinking of selling the company. He has no family to pass it on to, but he was still undecided. On a whim I asked him to give us first refusal. Since then I have been checking his company accounts and asking around about the state of the company. It is very profitable; they are about twice the size of us, but have mortgages outstanding on some of their garages."

"You have been busy. Have you taken it any further, like making an offer?" Rene was teasing him; he knew Mick would not have gone that far.

"No of course not, I would not do anything without talking to you first. Anyway, I still don't know if Duvall is serious about selling."

"Well there's one way to find out... phone him." Rene pointed to the phone.

"I'll ring him in the morning I don't want to talk business at this time of night."

Mick always arrived at the showroom in Bayeux by seven a.m. even though the workers didn't start until eight. He liked the quiet and it gave him time to plan out his day. Now that they had five locations he would generally spend one day at each to check on the work, and make sure that the quality was to his high standards. He had personally trained every manager they employed and all of them had been promoted from within the company. Today he was due to go to Cherbourg and would normally have left the office in time to arrive at about the same time the employees did. Today he would be late.

He waited until nine o'clock before putting the call in.

"Hello, may I speak to Mr Duval please?"

The girl on the other end of the line asked him to wait whilst she put the call through.

"Mr Furford? Duval speaking, what can I do for you?"

"You phoned yesterday and asked me to call you."

"Oh yes. You were asking about my intentions with regard to the company…well I'm prepared to listen to offers if you are still interested."

Mick took a sharp intake of breath. He could feel the excitement sweeping over him. He waited a second before replying, composing himself so as not to appear too keen.

"Yes, I am interested but will obviously need to see your accounts etc; can we set up a meeting?"

"I'll arrange for my accountants to send you a letter of confidentiality and, once signed, I will make all our records available to you. Please ring me once your people have seen the figures and we can arrange a meeting."

The phone went dead and Mick, still shaking with excitement walked across the corridor to Rene's office. Rene could see by the look on his face that he had something important to tell him and he knew exactly what that was.

Mick relayed the conversation he had just had with Duval.

"So Michael, you are pleased?"

"Yes, but are you?"

"Well I won't be able to answer that question until we know what it will cost." He laughed out loud. "I'm sure it won't come cheap but you'll find a way, of that I have no doubt." He winked at Mick as he said this.

Duval was as good as his word and a letter of confidentiality was delivered by hand that day. Mick's visit to Cherbourg was cut short by the phone call telling him the letter had arrived, and he quickly returned for him and Rene to sign the document, which they sent back by courier.

It took three weeks for the accountants to complete the due diligence on Duval's company and, at the end of their work, Anton De-Chamery, the senior partner in the firm of De-

Chamery and Sons, rang Mick to arrange a meeting with him and Rene.

"Michael, it's Anton, we are ready with all the information on Duval's, when would you like to get together?"

"You know me Anton, the sooner the better."

"Fine, I can be with you tomorrow morning at nine if that is convenient."

"I look forward to it."

Mick replaced the receiver and then called Rene on the internal intercom.

"Rene I have arranged a meeting, here, with Anton for tomorrow morning at nine to discuss the Duval takeover, is that okay with you?"

"Fine." The intercom clicked off, there was nothing more to be said until the meeting.

Mick did not change his routine and was at the works the following day at 7.30, making sure that the staff were all on their toes. He believed in setting an example and was convinced that their success was due to the respect that the workforce had for the owners.

Having signed some letters that were in his pending tray he settled down to wait for the accountants to arrive.

Dead on the stroke of nine the receptionist came on the line to say that his guests had arrived and she was sending them up.

Anton was a tall man who always wore a pinstriped suit which, if anything, exaggerated his height. He had a small pencil thin moustache and dark hair sleeked back with oil or cream, which gave it a shiny almost luminescent look to it. He entered the room and placing his brief case on the table turned to Mick and Rene and shook their hands vigorously. A young man in his twenties, obviously one of his juniors, followed him in and unloaded a pile of papers onto the desk next to Anton's briefcase.

Mick poured his guests coffee and they settled themselves around the table which was in the centre of the office.

Anton cleared his throat and was about to speak but Mick held up his hand.

"Anton before you start, we don't need you to go through all the details, we have complete faith in your judgment. You have never let us down in the past; we know you will have been exhaustive in your work. Please tell us two things, is the business viable and what is it worth?"

"Michael I anticipated your brevity and whilst you are correct, I could bore you for the next four hours going over the minutia of the Duval Company and we would reach the same conclusion. The business is viable but is highly leveraged and if you go ahead, you will have take on a considerable debt liability. Against that the land and premises are worth twice the amount of the debt. The company is profitable but not as profitable as yours. I would say that they are a lot less efficient and are overstaffed. However, they have a good name in the industry and a good credit rating. All in all, based on their last year's audited accounts, I would put a valuation of 750,000 francs on the company."

"Thank you Anton for your hard work. Rene and I need to talk over our next move. Can you tell me, if we decide to make an offer, will we be able to raise the capital from the banks?"

"Yes, your credit rating is excellent and the fact that you have always kept your bank informed of your monthly management accounts, will work in your favour. You have wisely not taken all the profits out of the company, but will have to liquidate your investments, as the bank will want you to put a substantial amount of cash into the pot."

"I see, but you are confident that we could proceed?"

"Definitely."

Mick and Rene shook hands with their accountant and walked with him to reception. The young junior, having collected all his papers, quickly followed them. He had been completely redundant through the whole of the meeting as Anton had suspected he might be, but having wanted to make sure that nothing had been missed, had brought him along just in case.

The two men made their way back to Rene's office.

"Well Michael what do you think or do I know already?" A mischievous twinkle appeared in the corner of his eye.

"How well you know me." Mick smiled back at the older man. "Yes I think we should make an offer for Duval Motors."

"We will be stretching ourselves further than we ever have before and if something goes wrong we could lose everything, are you prepared for that risk?"

Michael looked at his father-in-law. He totally respected Rene and if asked not to, would not go ahead.

"Rene I believe this is a golden opportunity, but if you say no I will respect your decision."

"Well I suppose we can always go back to repairing tractors and plough shares."

They were agreed, nothing more needed to be said.

That afternoon Mick rang Duval and asked if he could call and see him. He was, unfortunately, busy for the next couple of days and the earliest that they could meet was the following Monday. Mick agreed to be at his office first thing.

The next few days and all over the weekend Mick was like a bear with a sore head, he could think of nothing but the possible takeover. He hardly spoke to Giselle and had little time for the boys, which was out of character as he loved to take them to the park to play, weather permitting. Giselle knew not to complain, after all it would only be for a short time, and then the business would be complete, one way or the other.

Finally, Monday arrived and with a good luck kiss from Giselle he left for his appointment.

"Mr Duvall is expecting me," he said to the receptionist.

"Please take a seat, I will let him know you are here."

Mick resisted the urge to walk down the corridor to Duval's office, instead sitting down and pretending to read one of the trade magazines lying on the table.

After what seemed an age but was in fact only five minutes, the girl stood up and asked him to follow her to Mr Duval's office.

"Michael, how are you?" Duval took his hand. "Please sit down. Would you like coffee?"

He desperately wanted to say 'no, here's my offer now sign the papers, but knew he had to be patient.

"Thank you, black no sugar."

The girl poured the coffee then left the room.

"I'll come straight to the point; we are interested in making an offer for your company…"

"Good, good," Duval interrupted.

"It's not quite that straightforward. As I am sure you are aware, you have mortgages and borrowings that we would have to honour. Although the company is profitable overall, your profitability has declined during the last two years. Taking all things into account our valuation is 500,000 francs."

"Michael I too have had the company independently valued and their valuation is 800,000 francs, so I am afraid that unless you can make a revised offer I will have to look elsewhere."

"I have my partner's authority to move a little if necessary, can we meet half way?"

"No, I'm sorry but this is my pension, once the business is sold I intend to move to the south coast and retire. I will accept 750,000 francs but no less."

"Mr Duval I respect you as both a business man and a person, so I will not insult you by haggling further. I have to tell you that we cannot raise 750,000, so will have to withdraw our offer and wish you good luck with your sale."

"Michael I am truly sorry, I know you are an ambitious man and how well you have expanded your company, I also know you are a man of integrity and would not try and cheat me. I wish there was a way we could do business, for I feel the company would be in good hands if you took it over."

Michael sat there apparently deep in thought and after a few seconds leaned towards Duval.

"There might be a way…"

"Yes, what are you thinking?"

"As I said we could raise 650,000 francs now, but if you were prepared to wait for the balance, we could pay it to you over five years, which would give you an income as well as the lump sum, and give us the chance to earn the money to pay you. Naturally we would insist on you taking a charge against the company until the debt had been discharged."

Duval pushed his chair back and stood up and he held his hand out to Mick.

"Michael you have just bought Duval Motors, I wish you every success. I will get my solicitors to draw up the documents for you and Rene to sign."

Mick stood up and shook Duval's hand.

"Thank you, I hope you enjoy a long and happy retirement."

CHAPTER THIRTY-THREE

For the first time since Rene had invited him to go into the business he was scared. The contracts had been exchanged and they were now the proud owners of Duval Motors. The enlarged company had fourteen outlets and was the biggest franchise in Northern France. Mick's normal gung-ho approach and aura of invincibility hung heavy on his shoulders, for he realised if he failed this time it would mean ruin for the family.

"What is the matter, you do not look yourself?" Rene had appeared at the door to Mick's office. "It's only natural to have doubts, but if it helps, I believe in you and we can make it work."

"Can you read my mind?"

"Almost my friend, remember we have worked together these past five odd years and I think I know what makes you tick."

"Rene, have I gone too far this time? Has my ambition got the better of me?"

"No, no. Consider this, if the banks thought for one minute that it was a bad deal they would not have lent us the money. These people are not stupid and they certainly are not gamblers. We have a sound business and, with your drive, it will only improve."

"Thank you for your faith. I think I just needed some reassurance. Of course you are right it will work, it must work."

Rene slapped him on the back and laughed.

"It's my daughter I feel sorry for; I doubt that she will see much of you over the next few months."

Rene's prophecy proved to be correct, as Mick spent most of his time re-structuring the old Duval Company to fit in with the Remich Company blueprint. Each manager from the nine outlets were in turn sent to Bayeux for training and then returned to their depot to pass on the principles to their staff. Not all came up to scratch and those that didn't want to or couldn't were dispensed with. Mick had always found it hard to sack people and so gave them every opportunity to fit in before he finally resorted to the ultimate sanction.

Rene and Mick had agreed that they should keep the Duval name for that part of the enlarged company, after all part of the value that they had paid for was the reputation built up by Jacque Duval. It took most of the first year to complete the reorganisation, but during that time the enlarged company still managed to return a profit and pay the first instalment to Jacque Duval.

On the anniversary of the day they purchased Duval Motors, Rene had arranged for the three of them to go out to dinner to celebrate. Giselle had got Maria, a young girl in the village to baby sit, so they need not worry about the boys.

After the meal they moved into an adjacent room, where they were served with coffee and brandies.

"It's nice to have you two to myself for a change and perhaps Michael, now that you have finished your reorganisation, I will see more of you." Giselle held Mick's hand and smiled at him to let him know that she was not criticising, more requesting.

"Well, as a matter of fact, I've been thinking that we should move our head office to the Caen branch, after all it is the biggest by far and has a beautiful office suite that is not being used." Mick looked at Rene to see what reaction his statement had.

"I see your point but it is a long journey every day, and at my age I don't think I am up to it." Rene though knew it made sense.

"I agree with you. Anyway I think you should take things a little easier and enjoy your life more, after all you have worked hard and you're sixty, so why not wind down a little. You keep your office in Bayeux, we can communicate by phone and I can come over to you for any meetings."

"But you will see papa every evening anyway." Giselle could not see a problem.

"Yes my darling, but I think the time is also right for us to move and buy a house in Caen."

"But papa." Giselle looked shocked. "What about papa?"

Rene smiled and looked at Mick.

"You know then do you?"

"Know what? Will someone tell me what is going on?" Giselle's voice was getting louder and a few people in the room looked across at her.

"I think Rene should explain to you." Mick was grinning like a Cheshire cat.

"Giselle, I have met someone... a lady... she's a widow and we are well suited to each other..."

"What he's trying to say is that he is still young at heart and he's a man! So if we move to Caen, then Rene can have the house here and his young lady can move in." Mick could not stop grinning; he was enjoying seeing Rene's embarrassment.

"Young!" Giselle almost exploded.

"Giselle, take no notice of him, of course she's not young, she's fifty-six. Do you think I'm stupid? I would like you to meet her, I'm sure you will like her."

"Come on let's celebrate, I think this calls for a bottle of champagne." Mick called for the waiter and ordered the champagne.

The three raised their glasses and toasted the future, a future that would make them all very, very wealthy.

CHAPTER THIRTY-FOUR

The move to Caen took longer than anticipated. Mick wanted a much grander house, something befitting his status as a prominent businessman, somewhere he could bring important clients to entertain. Having established the principles for the enlarged company his next project was fleet sales.

Each outlet had a general manager and under him a sales manager, to look after new car sales and a service manager, to look after repairs and guarantee work. Now he wanted to tap into the lucrative market of company cars.

Even though they were still house hunting he had moved his office base to Caen and commuted everyday. He now took on the additional role of fleet sales director, and set about the task of courting companies large and small, in the areas that they had outlets, with a view to supplying their company cars.

Since the birth of the twins, Giselle had not worked in the company, preferring to stay at home and care for the children, but now that they were at school she had more time on her hands and wanted some sort of role. Mick realised that his wife was getting frustrated, but did not want her to work full time back in the company; however he wanted her to be happy. It suddenly came to him that they had not found a house, mainly because he had been too busy to look, so why not pass the house hunting to Giselle. She was the home maker anyway, with a flair for decoration and colour she would be perfect.

Feeling pleased with himself for thinking of the idea he broached the subject to Giselle.

"You want me to go house hunting... alone?"

"Yes... and no. I mean why don't you spend the time finding a place that you think we would be happy in, and then, when you have a short list, we can take a second look together."

"It means I am free to get on with the new fleet sales project and we can get together at weekends to go to those you have picked out."

"Well I suppose there is some sense in what you say, but what if you don't like what I choose?"

"My darling I know whatever you choose will be excellent, and anyway, you are the boss on the home front." They both laughed for he had never spoken a truer word.

When they told Rene he was delighted. He had been seeing his new lady friend for some time now and wanted desperately for her to move in with him, but she had said she would not feel comfortable until Mick and Giselle moved on.

Giselle did not waste any time and the very next day drove to Caen to visit all the estate agents she could find.

In the following weeks she visited endless houses, but they were either too small, or too far from schools, or in need of too much repair work. The job of house hunter that she had readily embraced was beginning to lose its glamour.

Mick was so wrapped up in his new venture that he hardly had time to notice her increasing frustration. He had two prospective deals with fairly large companies who wanted forty-five cars between them. The negotiations were proceeding, but in each case he was up against another company who were selling Peugeot cars. It came down to a straight fight on price and he had been advised that he was presently the dearer. He had to get back with a final proposal as they were making the decision in the next twenty-four hours.

"Hello, can I speak to Monsieur Chabal please." Mick had decided to take the bull by the horns and ring Chabal at the Citroen plant and see if he could help.

"Who's calling please?" the receptionist asked.

"Michael Furford," he replied.

"Please hold while I contact him."

He waited patiently until the call was put through.

"Michael, how are you?" Chabal's friendly voice boomed over the phone.

"Very well thank you, but I need your help."

"If it is in my power I am only too pleased to help you." Chabal had always held Mick in high esteem and followed his progress since their first meeting. "What can I do for you?"

"As you know I am trying to break into the fleet market and have two very interested parties, but I am up against a Peugeot franchisee and it looks like they might win the contract, they are cheaper than us."

"So what can I do to help?"

"Can you move on the price at all just for these deals?"

There was a pause; Chabal was obviously thinking it over.

"Michael, would an extra ten percent make the difference?"

"Yes I'm sure that would clinch the deal, thank you."

"Michael, I will get my secretary to confirm the new price structure and that will be the price for all future fleet deals that you negotiate."

"I don't know how to thank you, that is fantastic."

"No Michael, it is I who should thank you. Since you first came to us you have exceeded all our expectations, we are delighted to support you."

Mick put the phone down, then pressed the intercom.

"Juliette, please come to my office I need to dictate two very important letters."

By Saturday Mick had the fleet contracts secured and wanted to celebrate. He was convinced that he had made the right move by expanding into the fleet business, and although Rene had been a little apprehensive at first, he now fully backed the decision. There were more fleet contracts to be won but, for now, he had made the break through.

"I think I will take a couple of days off if that is okay with you Rene. Giselle has said that there are a few houses that I might like and after all I should show some interest."

Rene could not help smiling, he knew his daughter well and if she had got to the stage of picking out a 'few' houses to look at, he was certain she had one particular house in mind.

"Michael, of course I don't mind, you deserve a break... oh and the best of luck with the house hunting."

After spending the Sunday visiting six different houses, none of which fitted the bill, Mick began to wish that he had not agreed to have time off to accompany Giselle.

Monday morning Mick was up early as usual and, even though he was not going into the office, could not resist phoning to check that everything was in order. His secretary promised to call him if anything important turned up and reluctantly he settled down to wait for Giselle to return from dropping the boys at the school.

She had two houses left on her list to visit and Mick was not facing the prospect with any enthusiasm. The appointment at the first property was for ten fifteen, so as soon as she got back they left to drive to Caen.

The house was situated on the south side of the city near a park. The building could not been seen from the road, the entrance was guarded by large wrought iron gates that swung open to reveal a long drive. The young man from the estate agent was there to greet them and they followed his car along the sweeping drive up to the house.

Giselle gave a gasp as the house came into view, the literature that she had been sent did not do it justice. It was large and imposing with double wooden doors set back in a porch. The front wall by the porch had a beautiful wisteria climbing up the face of the building. The drive swept around an ornamental pond with a fountain playing on the water. To the right a garage, which looked big enough to take three cars, was separated from the main building by a pergola, which was straining under the weight of roses that filled its space.

Mick had to admit he was impressed, if the inside was as good then he could be interested.

The young estate agent opened the front door to let them in. The owners had already moved and the house was unoccupied. They entered into a large reception area with a staircase that swept round in a semi-circle onto a galleried landing. The area was open from floor to ceiling, taking in two floors. In the centre a large chandelier hung from an oak rafter. To right and left doors opened onto large rooms, which looked even bigger by the absence of furniture. One room had been used as a library and the other a sitting room. An archway under the return leg of the stairs led to further rooms. On the right an 'L' shaped room, the top of which returned behind the library they had first seen, was twice the size of the other reception rooms. A large fireplace, almost big enough to stand in, was on the wall that backed the library, its brick chimney breast dominating the area. The opposite wall had four large French windows that led onto a patio. Retracing their steps they went back into the hallway to the room behind the front sitting room. This had obviously been the dining room for, at the far end, there was a door and next to it a serving hatch. Giselle quickly walked the length of the room through this door to inspect the kitchen, she was not disappointed. The range was the main feature in the room with numerous cupboards arranged around it. On the wall facing the garden, under a large bay window, were not one but two sinks. There were two doors on the same wall, one led to the garden and the other to a washroom/boot room.

Giselle squeezed Mick's hand; he could feel her excitement and had to admit that he had a similar feeling.

They went back to the entrance and climbed the stairs; there was an air of grandeur about the stairs, which gave the whole house a 'presence'. The gallery, overlooking the entrance hall, led to left and right on the left side were three double bedrooms and a large bathroom. To the right there was a double bedroom and a smaller bathroom, and at the end of the landing the master bedroom, which was enormous. On the wall facing them at either end were two doors. On the right hand side the door opened into a bathroom and the left hand one opened into a dressing room, complete with hanging space and clothes drawers.

Giselle went to the bedroom window to look out to the garden. There were two acres of manicured lawns, trimmed hedges, rose bushes and even a pond with a waterfall.

"Darling it's perfect." She was like an excited schoolgirl on her first trip to the seaside.

"I agree it is perfect." He was already thinking that he could bring clients here and they would be impressed.

Mick turned to the young man.

"We'll have it."

"But sir I haven't told you how much yet," he stammered.

"I don't care how much it costs, we want it. Go back to your office and send all the papers to my solicitor."

The young man could not quite believe what was happening; all his other clients haggled over the price when buying, this Englishman was weird.

Mick and Giselle went downstairs and out into the garden, wandering around exploring all the nooks and crannies, not wanting to leave for fear of breaking the spell and finding the house was just a dream.

When they returned home they went straight to Rene's office to tell him the news, needless to say he was as happy for them as he was for himself. Now he could marry Marie-Sue.

CHAPTER THIRTY-FIVE

Jayne had finished putting up the Christmas decorations and was compiling her list of presents. She was looking forward to the holiday as, apart from phone calls, she had not spoken to the boys since the summer break. They had both asked if they could spend Christmas day with her and arranged to see their father the next day. To her surprise Nigel's relationship with Clare had survived their separation, and she had been pleased when he asked if Clare could join them for Christmas lunch. There would be six for lunch, as she always asked her mother and Granville, who it had to be admitted, was mellowing in his old age.

James, unlike his younger brother, had no steady girlfriend so would be staying with Jayne. Nigel spent any time away from university with Clare and stayed at her flat, but at least they would be a family for one day.

She was still pondering what to buy for Granville, who seemed to have everything he needed, when she heard the key turn in the front door.

"Mum, I'm home."

"I'm in the living room. Be a dear and make me a cup of tea would you?"

James came into the room and kissed his mother on the cheek.

"Christ, Mum, let me get in before you start bossing me about." He smiled, they always had this sort of banter and she knew he was not annoyed.

"Sorry, let me get you a drink you've just had a long drive and I've been sitting here doing nothing."

She got up and made her way to the kitchen and put the kettle on.

"Did you have a good journey?" she called out from the kitchen.

"Yes, no trouble at all."

Jayne reappeared with two steaming mugs of tea.

"So anything exciting been happening at college?"

"No nothing, just the same old routine, and you?"

"Same here. Since the summer's excitement with all your sleuthing it's been back to the grind... no I don't mean that. You know I love teaching."

He grinned, knowing exactly what she meant.

"I suppose you've heard nothing from the solicitor have you? That legacy has to be claimed by March or it will go to the hospital and there's only three months left."

"No, nothing, I think we can safely say that's the end of that."

"What does gran say about it all?"

"Not a lot. She hardly remembers him and is convinced he must have been killed in action."

"So that's it then."

The room went quiet, neither knowing quite what to say. For those few weeks in the summer Jayne's curiosity had been awoken and James had provided her with more information than she could have imagined, but there was no closure and she wondered if she would ever discover what really happened. All she had to link her to her father was the locket, the locket that she wore all the time.

CHAPTER THIRTY-SIX

Mick could not believe what a lucky man he was. True he had worked hard and in the early years had taken hardly any holidays, often packing Giselle and the boys off to the south coast with a promise to 'come down' at the weekends, a promise that never materialised. Now after eleven years of running the enlarged company and growing it organically, so that it was one of the countries leading suppliers of fleet cars for businesses, he finally felt that he could relax a little.

Peter and Oliver had finished their secondary schooling and it was time for them to decide on their careers. Mick had, from the day they were born, dreamed of the day when they would join him in the business, but Giselle wanted them to go to university and have the education that she had never been able to have.

It was time for a family get together to sort out this dilemma once and for all. Sunday lunch was the ideal time to discuss the future, for it was the one time in the week when they all sat down together.

"Well boys you know what I want to talk about don't you?" It was a rhetorical question because he did not wait for an answer. "Your mother and I want to know what you want to do for a living."

"Well I want to sell cars and I can't wait to start, I'm sure I can do as well as any of your sales team." Peter's confidence was legendary and yet somehow he never gave the impression of being arrogant.

"Dad, you know how I feel; I want to be an accountant and eventually be your finance director."

Mick was slightly taken aback, although he knew of Oliver's love of figures, he had never been as forceful as this.

"I see, so you have both made up your minds. You do know that your mother has always wanted you to go to university don't you?"

Giselle said nothing, waiting for their reply. They both looked down at their feet not wanting to say anything that might hurt her.

"Boys, as you know I have always wanted you both to join me in the company, especially now that Grandpa Rene has retired. We are a family business and I want the dynasty to continue."

Giselle gave a wry smile at this remark. She always found it slightly pretentious when Mick talked about 'the dynasty'.

"I have a suggestion to put to you which I would like you to consider carefully before making a decision. Oliver, if you want to be a financial director you will need to train and pass accountancy exams. If you are prepared to do this I suggest you become articled to Anton De-Chamery and then, once you are fully qualified, you can join the company. Peter, there is no doubt that you have a way with words and are very confident, all good attributes for a successful salesman, but I think you need to experience life a little to be able to empathise with the customers. I would ask that you apply for university and read social sciences, which will broaden your outlook and make you someone that people can talk to and trust."

A silence fell on the room; neither the boys nor Giselle had expected this. Giselle never ceased to wonder at Mick. She had been sure that he wanted the boys to join the company straight from school, and start in the workshops servicing cars as he had done. Instead he was keeping them grounded without losing their individual ambitions.

"Please go away and think on what I have said and tomorrow I want your answers. Now for the rest of the day let's finish our lunch and this excellent St Emillion." He laughed to break the tension and the three joined in.

Mick was not surprised when Oliver approached him next morning before he left for the office.

"I've thought over what you said and I agree. Being articled to an accountant of De-Chamery's standing would be much more useful than going to university. Can you fix it with him?"

Mick laughed, "I think we have enough leverage with Anton to get him on our side."

Mick left the house with a spring in his step, one down and one to go, but he did not think Peter would be as easy.

Mick returned home from work that evening wondering what Peter would say to him. He understood his son's eagerness to enter the business and was secretly pleased that he had this desire, but he knew that Giselle had set her heart on the boys going to university. She had accepted that Oliver being articled to Anton was virtually the same as studying for a degree, but still wanted Peter to enter some form of higher education.

Mick had come prepared. He had instructed his secretary to obtain details of courses offered by the Université de Caen Basse-Normandie. The university was one of the best in France having been rebuilt after the German bombing during the war, which had completely destroyed the original building. It had opened in 1957 and quickly achieved a deserved reputation in the academic world.

After the evening meal Mick broached the subject with Peter.

"Have you had any further thoughts about your future?"

"Yes, but I do not see the need to go to university. I am confident that I could sell your cars as well as any man you have now, so why do I need to wait, when I could be earning straight away?"

"Peter, do not let your confidence turn to arrogance, remember 'pride comes before a fall'. My employees have worked for many years developing their skills and even they make the occasional mistake. If you go in thinking that you will conquer the world I guarantee that something will go wrong."

"But I..."

"No, listen to me, you need to learn patience and to think twice and then act once. It is a lesson that your grandfather taught me many years ago. If you are not prepared to go to university then I am not prepared to offer you a job."

The words came like a bombshell and even Giselle was surprised at their severity.

"But you always said you wanted us both to work in the company, I don't understand." Peter looked from his father then to his mother incredulously.

"That is true, but on my terms. University first then I will offer you a position, otherwise you must make your own way."

Peter looked crestfallen. He had assumed that his father would have welcomed him with open arms, but now he had been given this ultimatum.

"What if I do go to university and then fail the course will you want me then?"

"Peter, the only way you will fail the course is if you deliberately set out to sabotage your studies. I don't think for one minute that you are a quitter so I am confident you will be successful. However, if by some chance you do not pass, but have tried your utmost, then I will be satisfied. I promise you; in that case there will be a position for you in the company."

"Then I concede and will enrol for the course, but in return will you let me work in the sales department during my vacations?"

Mick laughed.

"Peter you drive a hard bargain and that will stand you in good stead in the cut-throat world you want to enter. Yes, I accept your conditions for I know you are determined to prove me wrong."

The two hugged each other as if to seal the arrangement. Oliver had said nothing but was pleased that his brother had agreed, for he hoped one day they would be running the company together after their father eventually retired.

The boys left the table and went to the living room, leaving their parents still sitting around the dining table.

"You were very hard on Peter," Giselle spoke for the first time.

"It was you that wanted at least one of them to go to university."

"Yes, I know, but would you really have disowned him?"

"Giselle don't be silly, I was not disowning him, only trying to point out that you have to earn things in this life, they are not just given. You watch, he will be a better salesman and he has a desire to prove me wrong, which will drive him even harder."

"You are quite devious when you want to be aren't you?" She rose from her chair and walked around the table until she stood next to him. Bending down she kissed him. "I love you so much."

"But not as much as I love you."

CHAPTER THIRTY-SEVEN

Peter completed his three year university course and, as promised, Mick appointed him assistant to the sales manager at their main branch in Caen. He had knuckled down and had enjoyed university life. He was outgoing and loved all sports, so it was no surprise when he was picked for the college rugby team. A gifted scrum-half, in his second year he was appointed captain, a position he held for the final two years. Mick had kept his side of the bargain and Peter had spent all his holidays working in the sales department at 'Remich'. He had taken his fathers advice 'to watch and learn' and had curbed his natural instinct to take over, instead picking up little tips from the established salesmen.

Mick had been impressed and the feedback he got from his managers was all positive. Peter was liked by all and nobody felt that he was arrogant, a worry that Mick confessed might be the case.

Oliver had been articled to Anton for a period of four years and therefore could not join his brother at the company for a further twelve months. Mick made sure that his allowance was increased to match Peter's earnings during this final year, the last thing he wanted was any jealousy between the brothers. He need not have worried as Oliver had never been envious of Peter.

Once Oliver completed his final year he joined the company as assistant to the accounts manager, a much older man who had been with Mick since the early days and, although not as qualified as Oliver, what he lacked in exams he more than made up for in experience.

After the first week of Oliver joining his brother in the company, Mick took Giselle out to their favourite restaurant to celebrate.

"Well are you satisfied now that you have your 'dynasty' in place?" She smiled as she teased him.

"You know I am."

"What now then my darling? Do you intend to conquer France? Even the Germans struggled with that."

"Not conquer exactly... but I would like to expand further."

"Michael, are you never satisfied?"

"I'll let you know later when I get you to bed." He gave a dirty laugh.

"Be serious or you won't get the opportunity." She smiled back at him, knowing full well that he would.

"We have a blueprint that works, so why not enlarge the map, especially now that I have two lieutenants by my side?"

"Does this mean I will see even less of you?"

"No, I make you this promise: we will have at least four weeks away every year in the summer. In fact I think we should look at buying a property in the south, say around the Nice area. It would be good for Rene and Marie-Sue to use as a holiday home as well."

"I think that's a wonderful idea. When can we start looking?" She was joking and grinned at him.

"I think you should do what we did when we bought our present house. Spend some time looking for suitable properties, you could take Rene and Marie-Sue, and when you have sorted the wheat from the chaff, I will take a few days off and come with you to make the final choice. How does that sound?"

"It sounds fine, as fine as the opportunity that is coming your way later."

This time it was his turn to grin.

It took six months for Giselle to come up with three properties that she thought would be suitable, though there was one she liked most of all.

As promised, Mick took a few days off from work and they set off to drive to the coast, on a day that promised little relief from the constant rain that had been falling for most of the month. Fortunately, the more south they drove the better the weather and, by the time they reached their hotel on the

Promenade des Anglais, the sun was beating down. It was six thirty and after they had checked in and freshened up it was time for dinner. They had scheduled the next three days for visiting, having booked one visit each day, so that they would have time to enjoy the coast as well as the job in hand.

The first two houses they visited had not impressed Mick very much; although each had some features that he liked, neither had been quite right. Giselle had saved her own favourite till last and was sure Mick would fall in love with it as she had.

On the third day they set off from the hotel for their appointment with the agent. The property was only a couple of miles from Nice and just slightly inland. When they drove into the courtyard Mick was surprised to see that it was a single storied house, shaped in the form of a 'U' with the main building having two wings set around a beautiful swimming pool.

The entrance hall led straight across to a large living room, with French windows that gave access to the pool and gardens beyond. To the right wing of the 'U' housed the kitchen and a dining room, the latter also having doors opening onto the pool. The other wing provided three double bedrooms, each with its own en-suite shower and toilet. Mick instantly knew this was the one. The gardens were not so big that they could not be easily maintained, and there was sufficient room around the pool for sun beds. At the front of the house was a large garage, big enough for two cars and spare space on the drive for visitors' cars. To complete the picture, beyond the pool the gardens sloped down in a formal terracing. Standing at the top of the terracing Mick surveyed the view, it was like a picture. The land fell away so that there was an uninterrupted view of the sea. It was as if the coast had been drawn up into the hills to form the edge of the garden.

"Well what do you think?" Giselle looked at her husband and did not need an answer, the look on his face was sufficient. He was truly mesmerised.

"I think, my darling, that yet again you have excelled yourself, it's absolutely wonderful." He swung around and picked her up in his arms. "I do love you."

They drove back to Nice to complete the documentation for the purchase. The estate agent was surprised when Mick wrote a cheque for the full amount.

"I know you have to get all the papers signed and contracts drawn up, but if you would be kind enough to give me a receipt for my cheque, then you can pay it into your account and have the funds cleared ready for the exchange of contracts."

The agent made out the receipt; this had been the easiest sale of his life. He thought he must be the only estate agent that this had happened to, but then so had the young man in Caen many years before.

Giselle could not wait for them to return home and as soon as they got back to the hotel, was on the phone to Rene and Marie-Sue with the news.

When he took the call Rene smiled to himself. He had been with Giselle when she first saw the property and had known then that Mick stood no chance, as she had already made up her mind. Not that she had needed to persuade Mick, fortunately he too loved the house.

Once all the legal documents had been exchanged and she had received the keys, Giselle could not wait to start furnishing it. She knew that Mick would not want to be dragged around shops looking for furniture and fittings, so suggested that she and Marie-Sue should spend a few days at the house to complete the transformation. Mick had readily agreed to the plan, though this was still to be a joint venture, she would buy and he would pay!

They spent their first full holiday there that September. The boys were now too old to be on holiday with their parents, and anyway preferred the company of their friends, so they were alone. It was the honeymoon they never really had when they married.

Mick was surprised that he actually relaxed and switched off from the business. He was not pestered with calls so felt all was well back at the office, which in fact it was. Giselle had taken the precaution of telling his secretary that he did not want to be disturbed, unless something really important came up.

The four weeks passed quickly and Mick had to admit he felt a wrench to be leaving, but at least he felt refreshed with his batteries recharged and looking forward to the next challenge.

CHAPTER THIRTY-EIGHT

The twins were approaching their thirtieth birthday and Giselle wanted to have a big party to celebrate. They no longer lived with their parents having moved into separate flats in the centre of Caen. Oliver had a girlfriend, Chantelle, whom he had first met when he was articled to Anton. They were both accountants and shared a joint love of opera and ballet. She had been the only girl he had ever brought home, and Giselle had seen their love blossom over the years until, inevitably, they moved in together; sadly, as yet, there was no talk of marriage.

Where Oliver was introverted and shy, Peter was exactly the opposite. Giselle had lost count of the number of vivacious young women who had caught his eye, but he showed no signs of settling down. His flat was a typical bachelor pad, which to his mother always looked untidy. She could not understand how any girl in her right mind would want to visit it, let alone move in, but it did not seem to deter them. Peter had a smooth touch with the opposite sex and a lovely relaxed smile, which was disarming to old and young alike.

Giselle had suggested to Mick that they should hire a marquee for the party, as the garden was more than large enough and, to her surprise, he readily agreed. Mick was pleased she had suggested throwing a party, for there was something special he wanted to do for the boys' birthday.

Giselle had invited the twins around for Sunday lunch with, of course, Chantelle and Michelle who was Peter's latest love interest. After the meal Giselle told them of her plans for the party, saying that she thought they should cater for about a hundred and fifty guests, so would need a list from each of them to send to the printers for the invitation cards. Oliver was not over-enthusiastic about the party as he was not at ease amongst crowds, especially if there were people he did not know, but Chantelle thought it a splendid idea and soon persuaded him.

Peter, on the other hand, was effusive in his support, already working out in his mind what he might say when asked to speak.

Mick had kept quiet, just nodding in agreement with his wife as she outlined the arrangements. He was formulating his own little plan for the big day.

Giselle immersed herself in the organisation of the party. She had hired two marquees, one that held all the tables for the meal and another that linked to the main one, and which housed a dance floor and small stage for the band. The best caterers in Caen had been hired with no expense being spared on food and decorations for the event, each table sporting a large arrangement of flowers.

The day finally arrived with Giselle's prayers for a rain free day being answered. Guests entered the main marquee, each being announced by the M.C., before being introduced to Mick, Giselle and the twins. As requested, black tie and cocktail dresses were worn, much to Peter and Oliver's embarrassment, but it had been their mother's one stipulation.

Champagne and canapés flowed freely in the late sunshine of the evening, before the M.C. broke into the hubbub of chatter to announce that dinner was served.

The meal was a triumph; each course had been carefully selected by Giselle and cooked to perfection by the caterers. Mick had personally chosen the wines from his cellar. Over the years he had built up a collection of fine wines and had become something of a connoisseur.

The meal finished and, brandy glasses filled, it was time for Mick to address the guests.

"Ladies and gentlemen, friends, Rene, Marie-Sue welcome and thank you for being with us today to celebrate the thirtieth birthday of our sons Peter and Oliver." The applause interrupted him and he paused until it subsided. "As you all know, Giselle and I are very proud of them both, and we are now looking forward to the day when they will present us with some grandchildren." Laughter rippled around the room, joined in by Peter but not by Oliver, who blushed appreciably. "I am a very lucky man to have a beautiful wife and two sons who have followed me into the family business and, may I add, by their own efforts been instrumental in expanding the company. In recognition of their work, today I want to announce their appointment as directors and shareholders of the company. As from Monday next they will sit on the board of Remich."

There was loud applause from the guests as they all stood up to acknowledge the brothers. Peter and Oliver were stunned, but happy. They had not expected anything like this. Mick moved across to embrace them both in a big bear hug. Giselle had tears in her eyes as she, in turn, kissed them both, then turning to Mick, kissed him hard on the mouth.

"Thank you darling, what a wonderful surprise. How did you manage to keep that to yourself?"

He grinned at her, pleased with himself at the effect his words had had.

Peter was the first to recover some poise and took the microphone.

"On behalf of Oliver and myself I would like to thank my father for this wonderful news. We promise him that we will work hard to continue in the same tradition and with the same aims as he has always exhibited. I would also like to thank our mother for organising this wonderful party. Finally, thank you all, our friends, for joining us today to celebrate. Thank you."

There was more loud applause. Finally, the noise died down and the M.C. announced that there was dancing in the adjoining room.

Once the tables were cleared the caterers set up a bar in the main marquee, with every drink imaginable available.

At midnight, Giselle and Mick slipped away to the main house to go to bed, leaving the younger guests to continue the revelry until the early hours of the morning.

Rene and Marie-Sue had stayed overnight and came down for breakfast at nine o'clock. Giselle was in the kitchen and had already started the cooking. Mick was laying the table for the four of them. He knew Peter, Oliver and the girls would not be down for some time.

"Quite a surprise last night, when did you decide that?" Rene enquired.

"I've been thinking for some time that they were ready and when Giselle decided to have a big party, it just seemed natural to combine the two."

"I think you are right. The company is getting so big now it needs more than one person to control it. I have been worried that you were stretching yourself too thin. They are two good boys, you must be very proud."

"Yes, as are you Rene."

Rene smiled. It was true he was very proud. His mind went back to when they first met and Mick came to his small garage to help. They had all come a long way since then.

CHAPTER THIRTY-NINE

It was December 24th 1983. Giselle was preparing the vegetables for Christmas lunch the next day. She liked to be well prepared rather than leave everything to the last minute, and anyway there was Mass in the morning, so the more she did today the better. Giselle liked nothing more than having all the family around her at Christmas and this year would be extra special. It was the first Christmas for little Edith, who was now ten months old. Oliver and Chantelle had finally married two years earlier and now had a pretty little girl, who was the apple of her doting grandfather's eye. In addition, Peter would be with them, though as yet they did not know who he would be bringing, and Rene and Marie-Sue were due later that day to stay for a few days.

As always, Giselle had covered the house in decorations and a huge Christmas tree stood in the corner of the living room, surrounded by a mountain of presents. The only thing missing was snow. The weather had not been kind as it had been raining constantly and that, coupled with the high winds, had blown away any chances of a white Christmas. Giselle was not going to let the poor weather dampen her spirits, and she had been pleased when Mick had said that he would start the holiday period a few days before the normal shutdown. In fairness, Christmas was not a busy time, certainly not on the sales side, and he had told his service managers, if they worked on the Saturday prior to the holiday to ensure all the work was finished, they could break up on the 23rd, plus being paid extra for the overtime.

Mick had helped Giselle with putting up the decorations, but drew the line at helping in the kitchen, his field of expertise extended to all things practical not domestic. He had never taken up golf or indeed any hobbies other than his interest in cars. His pride and joy was his Ferrari, a bright red monster that he had bought second-hand from a business associate. It was second-hand only in the fact that it was one year old when he purchased it. He adored the car. Giselle had joked that, had the Ferrari been a woman, she could have divorced him for being unfaithful to her, he loved it that much. At weekends, after they had returned from Mass, he would ease the car out of its garage, head for the countryside and speed up and down the lanes, taking pleasure in the throaty roar that burst from the exhaust. The locals knew when not to take their constitutionals!

There was more to his passion than just driving, he had stripped the engine down and painstakingly cleaned and polished every part, tuning the engine until he had the maximum power that could be wrung from it. Once every month he would service the car, whether it was needed or not, as part of the pleasure of owning such a high precision machine was just tinkering with the engine, coaxing even more out of it.

With Giselle busy in the kitchen he had taken the opportunity to spend some time with his 'mistress'. When he first bought the Ferrari he had a pit built in the floor of the garage, so that he could work under the car without any difficulty; he was busy oiling the engine when he heard a voice in the distance.

"I'm under the car," he shouted, though he could not make out whose voice it was.

"Michael."

This time he recognised Giselle's call and putting down the oil can, walked the length of the pit to the steps that brought him back up to the floor level of the garage.

"Be with you in a minute, just let me wipe my hands," he shouted back towards the house.

Having cleaned most of the oil and grease from his hands he walked towards the open doors of the garage. The doors had been swinging backwards and forwards in the wind and he had tried to wedge them in the open position to stop them banging. He was thinking that he must remember to check the air pressure on the front tyre, which he had noticed looked slightly flatter than the others; he was not looking where he was going when it happened. As he walked through the doorway a sudden gust of wind whipped the door from its temporary anchor, slamming it shut at that very moment. Before he could move, the door slammed into him knocking him backwards. Losing his balance he fell back with a thud, cracking his head on the bonnet of the Ferrari. Everything went black as he lost consciousness.

Giselle wondered where on earth he had got to, surely it didn't take all this time to wipe a pair of dirty hands. She needed him to lift the turkey into the cold room for storage overnight. She had insisted on having a turkey, weighing nine kilos, which even she had to admit was huge, and would probably feed sixteen let alone eight. When he did not reply to her third shout, she strode out of the kitchen determined to give him a piece of her mind. Playing with his toy was one thing, repeatedly ignoring her was another.

As she approached the garage she saw him lying, slumped in front of the car, his head angled to one side. Letting out a scream she ran to where he lay, frightened at what might have happened. Propping him up against the radiator she felt for his pulse, which she found to her relief was beating strongly. She lifted the lids of his eyes, but there was no sign of recognition. She was torn between not wanting to leave him and going to find help. He was breathing, so she decided that it would be best to ring the doctor for advice. She ran back to the house and phoned their doctor, who was not only the family physician but also a friend.

"Charles, I need your help. Michael has had an accident, he's unconscious and I can't move him. What should I do?" The words came out in a breathless rush, her heart racing as if the faster she spoke the quicker would come the help.

"Calm down, have you taken his pulse and is he breathing normally?" He waited for the reply. "Good then do not panic I will be there straight away. Go back to him with a cold compress and put it on the area where you think he hit his head. Take a glass of water and if he comes round let him sip it, but do not let him drink to deeply, we don't want him to choke. I will be with you in ten minutes."

The phone went dead, Giselle followed his instructions and took the compress and water out to where Mick still lay. Gently she felt his head until she found the large bump that had already developed on the back of the skull just above the neck. Taking as much care as possible so as not to move him, she placed the compress against the lump. He gave a slight groan as if the compress had magically woken him. Slowly he opened his eyes and looked at her, but said nothing. For a moment the fear gripped her that he could not speak, but she breathed a sigh of relief as he groaned, although not saying anything. As Charles had instructed, she held the water to his mouth and tipped the mug so that a little of the liquid ran down his lips, but most spilled over and down onto his chin.

She turned as the sound of a car pulled onto the drive and Charles appeared from its open door. Picking up his medical bag he ran quickly to the open garage where Mick lay propped against his car. Reaching into the bag he withdrew a small bottle of smelling salts and waived them under his nose. Mick gave another groan but this time his eyes opened slowly.

"I don't think it's too serious, just a nasty bang by the look of it, which knocked him out. He should be fine in a few minutes, well, fine except for a sore head." He gave Giselle a little smile of encouragement; he could see that she was still shocked by what had happened.

After a few minutes he helped Mick to his feet and with Giselle's help, they supported him as he tentatively shuffled towards the house.

"I think you should rest for a while and take these painkillers every four hours until the pain eases." He handed Giselle a bottle of tablets which she took into the kitchen, returning with two and a glass of water.

Mick had come round now but was feeling unsteady; the pain in his head was so bad that he felt sick. Charles helped him to the sofa and with a cushion supporting his head he stretched out and soon fell asleep.

"Don't worry I don't think he has done any serious damage, but if he feels worse ring me straight away and I'll be right out, otherwise let him sleep as long has he needs. I hope this won't spoil your Christmas, did you have any jobs for him to do?" He smiled again; it could not be that bad she thought.

Mick was still fast asleep when Rene and Marie-Sue arrived and in fact did not stir until late that evening. The three of them had kept clear of the living room and were ensconced in the kitchen, catching up on the latest happenings in Bayeux, when Giselle heard him shout.

"Giselle, Giselle."

She ran into the living room worried that there was a problem.

"What is it, are you in pain? Do you need more tablets?"

"No, yes... I mean yes my head aches but that's not why I called. Giselle... I remember!"

"Remember what?"

"Before we met... I remember being in England... I had a friend Tommy... He couldn't come on the invasion... He'd been injured. It's all coming back to me."

"My God! I never thought your memory would return. Are you sure it's not just an hallucination?"

"I am sure we were close friends, we would have been together if he hadn't lost his leg in an accident."

Rene and Marie-Sue had followed Giselle into the room and were listening intently, as surprised as Giselle by his words.

"I lived in Wolverhampton with my father, my mother had died earlier. He had a garage repairing cars like you Rene, and I used to help him as a boy during school holidays."

"Well that explains how you knew so much about cars and engines when you came to work for me," Rene interrupted.

"I wonder if he is still alive, he'd be an old man now." Rene coughed and frowned at this remark. "He will no doubt think I'm dead after all this time. I should go to England in the New Year and try and make contact."

"We'll go together; I've always wanted to visit England. I can test just how good my English is." Giselle felt a sense of relief that Mick seemed to have recovered from his accident without any after-effects, other than he had regained his memory. The fall, she assumed, had jolted something in his brain.

They did not stay up late, tomorrow would be a busy day with all the family and Giselle had demanded that he needed to rest fully, even though he insisted that he would be fine.

As he pulled up the bed sheets around his neck he turned to Giselle.

"There's something I did not mention downstairs, not in front of Rene, I wanted to tell you first."

"What?" She looked at him quizzically.

"In 1941 I met a girl in a city called Coventry; I was stationed nearby, and had gone to a dance with Tommy. We met two girls and after the dance took them home. Well…I…stayed with her for a few hours. We were attracted to each other. It was the middle of the war. Coventry was being bombed regularly."

He was finding it difficult to speak, the words coming out in short sentences, as if being dragged from him under interrogation.

"Life was cheap …no one knew if they would be killed the next day…"

"You made love to her." Giselle interrupted him, it was not a question it was a statement.

"Yes."

"So, I'm not jealous, I did not even know you then. These things happen."

"There's more. She had a baby, a little girl called Jayne. She came to my camp to tell me. I was away on manoeuvres, so she left a message with my C.O. that, if I wanted to see the baby, to contact her."

"And did you see the baby?"

"No. I thought that it would be better to wait until the war was over, that way if I got killed she would never have known me. I thought the war would only last another year, but of course it didn't and, well, you know the rest."

"I see, so somewhere in England you have a daughter who you have never seen and who probably doesn't know anything about you. Don't you think it would be best if you left it that way?"

"Maybe you are right, it's forty odd years ago, she most likely has her own family now." He put his arms round her and kissed her softly. "I do love you."

She squeezed him.

"Good night my darling. Let's look forward to a great family Christmas and then we can plan our trip to England... okay?"

"Yes, goodnight."

CHAPTER FORTY

The plane touched down at Heathrow and taxied slowly to the terminal. Mick sat there patiently waiting for the seat belt light to be switched off, as the light went off everyone on the plane stirred into life, standing in the aisles, reaching up to the overhead lockers to retrieve their hand luggage. Mick and Giselle did not move. What was the point in rushing, they would only have to wait in the baggage reclaim hall for the suitcases to be unloaded? Eventually the passengers shuffled down the gangway and into the terminal building. Mick and Giselle were the last to leave the plane.

He had never been to Heathrow in his life. He had flown from Paris to many destinations in Europe and even to America, but he had never been back to England. They had decided to spend a week, combining a visit to Wolverhampton with a few days sightseeing in London, something Giselle had always wanted to do.

When they finally collected their suitcases and cleared immigration, they made their way to the taxi rank outside. Although there was a queue, a steady stream of taxies quickly cleared the waiting travellers. The car pulled up beside Mick and he and Giselle got in whilst the driver loaded their bags.

"Where to, governor?"

"Claridges, please."

They settled back in the seat as the car pulled away and sped into the traffic heading into the city. Mick had picked one of the most expensive hotels he could find; he wanted this to be a special trip for Giselle.

At the hotel the porter collected their bags and they followed him through the foyer to reception.

"I have a reservation, the name is Furford."

The girl on the desk looked up at him and pushed a form forward for him to fill in his details. "Bien venue, Monsieur."

He was taken aback. He had spoken to her in English but she had assumed that he was French. After forty years he must have assimilated a French accent, to the extent that even speaking English it was with a French inflection in his voice. He looked at Giselle who had a silly grin on her face.

"They think you're French," she whispered.

Having checked in, they were shown to their room by the same porter who had first carried their cases and Mick duly rewarded him.

"Let's unpack, shower and change, then we can plan our itinerary over cocktails in the bar, followed by dinner here in the hotel restaurant. Does that sound okay?"

Giselle nodded her head in agreement.

The waiter brought their drinks to a table in the corner, where they sat in deep leather chairs at right angles to each other, so they could talk but also watch the other customers as they passed to and fro in the bar.

"I thought we could set off about nine tomorrow morning catching the train from Euston, which will take us straight through to Wolverhampton, it's about two hours, then get a taxi to where my father's garage is. He may not be there but they should be able to tell me where to find him. If we meet up with him we can always find a hotel in the city and stop overnight to spend some time together."

"How old would he be now?"

"In his eighties, so I guess he would have sold the garage and be retired, but I still think it's the best place to start."

They had just finished their drinks when the Maître d' from the restaurant came in to tell them their table was ready.

Next morning they rose bright and early, Mick feeling quite excited by the thought of seeing his father after all that time, a father he did not know existed until the bang on the head had restored his memory. The taxi dropped them off at Euston, with five minutes to spare before the train departed to the Midlands. The countryside flew past them as the express carved its way northwards. Although, being February, the weather was cold, at least it was a bright sunny day and Giselle spent the journey glued to the window.

They exited the train station and hailed a cab. Mick felt totally lost, the city was nothing like the one he remembered. New buildings had sprung up everywhere he looked. He gave the cabbie the address of the garage in Chester Road. The taxi swung out from the station forecourt and through the city. He did not recognise anything until the cab finally turned into Chester Road. Most of the original street had survived although improvements had obviously been made to some of the pre-war properties. The taxi pulled to a halt outside a plot of ground that was flattened, weeds springing up through the rubble that lay strewn all over the site. A chain-link fence formed a barrier to the pavement.

"This it mate?" The taxi driver pulled the brake up as the car came to a halt.

Mick realised this was where the garage had stood; he remembered that it was next to the hardware store of old Ivor Monger.

"Can you wait here while I just pop into the store and find out what happened to the garage?" he asked the cabbie, then turned to Giselle. "Will you wait in the car, I won't be a minute?"

The taxi driver kept the engine running, the meter ticking continually, adding extra pounds to the fare.

Mick walked into the shop. There were no customers and the man behind the counter did not rush to greet him.

"Is Ivor about?"

"Christ! You're a bit out of date mate. He retired ages ago, I'm his son; can I help you?"

"Yes, can you tell me what happened to the garage next door and the owner, Mr Furford?"

"I'm afraid the garage burnt down and not long after Mr Furford died. He'd lost his wife and then his son went to war and he never saw him again, so we think he just gave up, lost the will to live."

Mick felt a lump in his throat and had to fight back the tears.

"Why do you ask anyway, did you know the family?

"I'm his son, Mick Furford," he replied flatly.

"Oh bloody hell, I'm sorry. You were only young and I was a kid when you left. I'm so sorry, I just hit you with it. Can I get you a drink of anything?"

"No… no… it's okay… You weren't to know."

"It's strange you coming in like this I had a young man here in the summer, he was asking about your father. He said he was a relation."

"What!"

"Yes, he was trying to trace his relations, asked about the solicitors that handled the fire claim. I told him who they were, Davies and Renshaw."

"Do you have their address?"

"Yes, 21 Lower Street. I did have the lad's phone number but I've thrown it away now. His name's James."

Mick thanked him for all his help and returned to the waiting cab, which by now had doubled the fare.

"What's wrong, you look as white as a sheet? What happened?" Giselle was concerned; he looked shaken by whatever he had discovered.

"We need to go to some solicitors, I'll explain as we go."

He got into the back of the cab and gave the driver the address of Davies and Renshaw. The taxi pulled away from the kerb and Mick nestled into the seat. He squeezed Giselle's hand as if drawing some inner strength from her.

"My father is dead… apparently there was a fire that burnt the garage down and he never got over it… lost his will to live. It was thirty years ago." The words came out in a disjointed fashion, as blank statements of fact, as though he was reading from a text.

"Oh Michael I'm so sorry, we have come all this way for nothing then?"

"Well not exactly, that's the strange thing, the man in the store said that a young man was enquiring about my father last summer, he claimed that he was a relation. He might be related to me. Anyway, the lad was given the name of the solicitor that we are going to now, so we can find out who he is."

Giselle said nothing, not fully understanding what was happening. The car fell silent for the rest of the journey.

It was not long before the taxi pulled up outside the offices of the solicitors. Mick paid the driver and thanked him with a generous tip. It was with some trepidation that they entered the building.

The receptionist looked up as they entered.

"Good afternoon, can I help you?"

"I hope so. I don't have an appointment but I was wondering if I could speak to the gentleman who handled my father's affairs when he died. It was thirty years ago if that is any help."

"Can I take your name please?"

"Oh, of course I'm sorry; it's Furford, Michael Furford. My father's name was Richard Furford."

"Please take a seat and I'll enquire."

Mick and Giselle sat on the leather chesterfield to the right of the reception desk and waited.

"Mr Furford."

It had been only a couple of minutes since she had placed the call.

"I've spoken to Mr Renshaw and he confirms that he handled Mr Furford's affairs. If you would like to make an appointment he will be happy to see you, say next Thursday?"

"I live in France and am only in England for two days, and I'm staying at Claridges in London. I would really appreciate it if he could spare me a few moments, otherwise I will have to fly back into England again." The lie about staying just two days came easily. He certainly didn't want to trek all this way again when it could be done now, and he was used to getting his own way.

"I'll try." She picked up the phone and rang through to the partner's office, explaining the predicament.

"Under the circumstances, Mr Renshaw will see you now, but he can only spare ten minutes."

Mick smiled.

"Thank you very much, that is very kind of him."

Moments later a young woman appeared from the far door and asked them to follow her. She led them down a short corridor at the end of which was a glass panelled door with the words 'David Renshaw' printed on it. She knocked, opened the door and they followed her in.

David Renshaw was not much older than Mick, a tall lean man who stood up and held out his hand to greet them.

"Mr Furford? Pleased to meet you." He looked enquiringly at Giselle.

"Pleased to meet you. This is my wife, Giselle."

Renshaw shook her hand and indicated them to sit down.

"Perhaps I should explain why I am here. I was in the army during the war, part of the D-Day invasion. Well, I was injured during our advance to liberate Caen and Giselle and her father cared for me. The problem was that as well as temporary paralysis of my legs, which lasted a year, I also lost my memory. In fact I have had no recollection of my life prior to that day in 1944. It was as if my life started then and I have lived and worked in France ever since. Then on Christmas Eve, just past, I had an accident and was concussed. When I came round my memory had returned. Obviously I wanted to see my father and we have flown over for that purpose. I have learnt today that my father sadly died shortly after a fire at his place of work, and I have come to you to see if you can tell me what happened."

Renshaw had listened intently to the story not interrupting, though there were questions he would need to ask.

"That would explain why you have a French accent. I must admit when you spoke I could not see how you could be Richard Furford's son if you were a Frenchman. I was a young man when the fire happened and our practice helped your father negotiate a settlement from the insurance company after the fire. It was odd because, soon after the claim had been settled, your father came to me asking to make a will, it was as if he knew something might happen. The will was the strangest one I have ever prepared. He left everything to you, but in the form of an investment, the yearly profits from which should be passed to the hospital that treated your mother, until you returned to claim it. He always believed that you had not died and one day you would return. The investment was not a large amount, £50,000, but at today's valuation I would guess it is worth eight to ten times that figure. There was one final stipulation; if you had not claimed it within thirty years of the date of the will, the capital sum would go to the hospital. Interestingly, that date expires on the thirty-first of March this year, in one month in fact."

Mick was taken aback, he had not expected a legacy, all he had wanted, hoped for, was to find his father.

Renshaw looked at him.

"Are you alright? You look a little pale, can I get you a glass of water?"

"No, thank you I'm fine; it's just a bit of a shock."

"Look I'm sorry to ask but do you have some means of identification with you?"

"No, my papers are back in the hotel safe."

"Would these be of any use?" Giselle passed a small bundle of old papers held together with an elastic band, to the solicitor. "They are Michael's identification papers he had with him when he was in the army. I have kept them as a memento from when we first met and I brought them with me to show his father. I thought he might like them as a keepsake."

Renshaw examined the papers and the photograph which was of a man forty years younger, but still discernable as Mick.

"Yes those are fine, may I take copies? He rang for his secretary who took the papers, returning within minutes with the originals. With your permission I will file for probate immediately, it should be granted in a couple of weeks."

"There was something else I wanted to ask you. I understand that a young man called James was enquiring after my father and that he came to see you last summer. Do you know anything about him?"

"Oh yes, I had quite forgotten about him. His name is James Harris and he said that he was trying to trace his grandfather, who he believed was you. I promised to contact him if anyone ever claimed the inheritance. Would you have any objections to me speaking to him?"

"No, but I would like to contact him myself. Do you have a number or address? By the way, did he tell you his mother's name by any chance?"

"Yes, Jayne."

Mick let out a gasp. It must be his daughter.

Renshaw passed Mick a piece of paper with two phone numbers written on it. Next to the first was 'home' and the second 'university'.

Mick stood up and thanked the solicitor, before reaching into his wallet and passing him his business card with his home address scrawled on the back. Renshaw's eyebrows rose when he read the card.

'Michael Furford Managing Director Remich Cars Ltd. (27 Branches in Northern France)'

"Good day Mr Furford, Mrs Furford, I will be in touch."

When they returned to the reception desk Mick asked the girl if she would be kind enough to call a taxi to take them to the station. Within three hours they were back in their room at Claridges.

They had hardly spoken on the journey back from Wolverhampton. Mick had been deep in thought. Since he had recovered his memory everything seemed to be moving so quickly. He knew that Giselle had felt it better not to look for his daughter, and he had agreed that, after all this time, it would probably be best to let sleeping dogs lie. Now things were different, she, or at least her son, had been looking for him and he was drawn to finding the missing piece from his life.

"Giselle I'm going to ring this boy, James, and talk to him, maybe arrange a meeting. You don't mind do you?"

"Of course I don't. It would have been different if he had not made enquiries after you, but yes, you must contact him."

He knew why he loved her so much, she was kind and understanding and totally selfless. He withdrew the piece of paper with the telephone numbers on and went to the telephone by the side of the bed. The receptionist answered and he asked for an outside line. He waited until the dialling tone came on then dialled the first number. The phone rang for some time without answer. He redialled, this time entering the second number he had been given. Again the phone rang three or four times but was then picked up a voice answering with….

"Hello, James Harris speaking."

"James, I'm Michael Furford, I believe you have been trying to trace me."

"You're Mick Furford? But I thought you had died in the war. You were posted missing presumed dead. This isn't a joke is it, because, if it is, it's in very bad taste?"

"No, no I'm serious. It's a long story and we need to meet so that I can explain. I live in France and am over for a couple of days can, we get together?"

"Well yes, I suppose so, where do you want to meet and when?"

"Tomorrow is Saturday. Can you get a train to London? I'm staying at Claridges. I will reimburse you the fares, if you could meet me at the hotel. If you could get here about midday we can talk over lunch. Just so that you know it is not a hoax, I got your number from Davies and Renshaw, my father's solicitors."

"Yes I remember them, I visited them last summer."

"Fine, I will see you tomorrow then. Come to the hotel and ask the receptionist to ring my room, it's number 357. Bye for now."

Mick looked at Giselle.

"Tomorrow will be interesting to say the least."

She put her arms around him and kissed him.

"Now, let's eat, I'm famished."

Saturday morning Mick rose early and after breakfast suggested that they go for a stroll along Piccadilly and past Buckingham Palace. He needed to be occupied for he had not slept well, his mind going over what he would say to the grandson he had never met.

It was cold but bright, the sun cascading through the bare branches of the trees, as they made their way through Green Park towards the Palace. They were well wrapped up in their overcoats and Giselle was glad that she had brought her thick fur boots, though after half an hour's brisk walking, only the tips of their fingers felt cold, the heat generated from their bodies providing a warm insulation.

Mick looked at his watch. It was eleven thirty and he wanted to make sure they were back in time for James. He flagged down a passing black cab and they sped back to the hotel, the return journey taking only five minutes. As he passed reception he stopped to tell the girl on duty that he was expecting a visitor, and would she ring him when he arrived.

Once inside their room he took a brandy from the Mini bar. He felt more nervous than he ever had, even when he had been negotiating a large contract.

"Calm down, it will be fine. This is not an ordeal it's a reunion." Giselle grinned at him, trying to break the tension that she knew was building up inside him.

"Yes, I know. I just feel strange, not sure what to say."

"Just tell him the truth, what else is there to say?"

The phone rang. For a moment he stared at it not moving. Giselle walked across the room and picked it up.

"Yes, fine, tell him we will be right down." She replaced the receiver. "Come on he's in the foyer."

They took the lift down, crossed to the reception desk and asked for the gentleman who had just called them. The girl pointed to a young man sitting by a large pillar, a briefcase leaning up against the leg of the chair.

Mick and Giselle walked across to him.

"James? I'm Michael Furford and this is my wife Giselle."

"Pleased to meet you both." James looked as nervous as Mick felt.

"Would you like a drink before we eat?"

"Thanks, a lager would be fine."

Mick called the waiter over and ordered two brandies and a lager.

"I thought we could eat here at the hotel is that okay?"

"Great, thank you."

"Let's go through to the dining room then."

They were led to their table and opted for the set lunch. Once the order had been taken and the wine served, they passed a few pleasantries about the weather and how good it was for the time of the year. Both men were feeling the strain, going through the formalities, not being able to relax. It was Giselle who came to the rescue.

"Hey you two, you might be strangers but you're related! Relax and enjoy." She smiled at them both and it seemed to do the trick, for they both spoke at the same time.

"Sorry, please carry on, but what do I call you, Mr Furford, granddad, Mick?"

Mick laughed, he had not given it a thought.

"I think granddad or grandpa would be very nice, but let me tell you a little of what has happened over these last forty years."

Mick related how he had met James's grandmother during the war, and although she had left a message telling him about his daughter Jayne, he had not wanted to see her until after the war, just in case anything happened to him. When the invasion came he had left a locket with his friend Tommy, to pass on to Jayne in the event of his not coming back.

"I know, my mother has the locket." James could not help interrupting. "Your friend Tommy was killed in an accident and the locket was left in his will. The solicitors tracked Mum down to give it to her."

"Oh I see, well I'm glad she got it. Poor old Tommy, it seems all the people I would like to see again are gone. Anyway, back to my story. We landed on the Normandy beaches on D-Day and were heading for Caen when our convoy was hit by Stukas. My Jeep was shot up but luckily I was thrown from the vehicle into a field. I lay there for about a day before Giselle's father found me and took me back to his house. I was suffering from paralysis of the legs and loss of memory. Giselle nursed me back to health, and after about a year I got the use of my legs back, but no memory recall. Giselle and I married and, with her father, we built up a business repairing cars and then expanded into selling new cars."

"Your grandfather is too modest. He has built up quite an empire, and Remich Motors is the biggest franchisee in northern France for Citroen cars." Giselle could not help but sing his praises.

"So as far as my memory told me, I had no other life but my new one in France. Giselle taught me to speak French and now it is my first language."

"But if you are over here asking about your father you must be able to remember." James was curious to say the least.

"On Christmas Eve I was fiddling with my car, it's my hobby, and I had an accident. The garage door blew in my face and knocked me backwards and I struck my head on the grill of the car. I passed out for a while, but when I came to I could remember the past. The doctor said that the shock had trigged a response in my brain that released all that had previously been locked away."

"So that's why no one has heard anything from you until now."

"When I recovered my memory, I wanted to come to England to see my father, but as you know he passed away some time ago. But tell me, how did you find out where my father was, I never mentioned his name to your grandmother."

"It started when my mother received the locket. Your friend had left instructions in his will to pass it to Mick Furford's daughter, giving her last whereabouts as Coventry and her name as Jayne Brown. Apparently they had detectives chasing all round the city before they finally contacted Mum. I was home, on holiday from university and we examined the locket. Well, to cut a long story short, I worked out from the inscription who Sir George Davenport was and did a bit of digging. I found a retired reporter who had worked on the local newspaper in Worcester at the time, and learnt that Sir George was in fact your biological father. Did you know that?"

"Yes, my mother told me just before she died, but I always looked on Richard Furford as my father."

"Well, I followed the trail via your mother to Wolverhampton, and went to see Mr Furford. Unfortunately, as you know, he had passed away and that, as far as I could see, was the end. My mother had hoped that we would find you but the trail went dead. Strange though, she has always said she thought you were alive. She must have sixth sense."

"I would like to meet her, do you think she would see me? Have you told her of this meeting?"

"No I wanted to meet you first and not get her hopes up in case you did not want to see her."

"Of course I want to see her."

James was pleased and knew that Jayne would be too.

"There's something else. I assume that Renshaw told you about the will?" Mick nodded. "Well there is another will; your biological father, Sir George, left you an inheritance of £500,000, which at today's figures would be worth double that."

"How do you know all this?"

James smiled, "My ex-reporter had found out and passed the information to me. He gave me the name of Sir George's solicitors. They are Hodgson Smyth & Co of High Street Worcester. You should contact them."

"I will, don't worry."

They finished their lunch both relaxed now, Mick asking about Jayne and Nigel, wanting to know all about their lives in England. In no time it was three o'clock and James, looking at his watch, said he would have to leave, otherwise he would miss his train. Mick gave him a hundred pounds, which would more than pay for the train fare but insisted on James taking it.

"Buy you mother a bottle of Champagne if you have enough left over. Please ring me on this number and I will arrange to fly over to meet your mum." He gave James one of his business cards with his private number quickly added to the business ones.

They waved James goodbye as he got in the taxi to take him to the station.

"Well what do you think of that?" Giselle asked as they walked back towards the lift.

"Think of what, James do you mean?"

"No, what he told you about your real father leaving you all that money. Are you going to contact the solicitors?"

"Yes I'll ring them on Monday and see if we can meet them before we fly home, but for now let's just enjoy London. You know, I came once with my mother and father to visit the science museum. I was about thirteen and everything looked so big and imposing. Of course, since the war, there has been a lot of rebuilding. It all looks so modern now. Would you like to see a show tonight? I'm sure the concierge will be able to get tickets even at the last minute. You go up and get ready while I ask the question. I'll be up straight away."

Without waiting for an answer he turned and walked to the concierge. Giselle caught the lift and by the time he entered the bedroom she was already showered.

The weekend flew by. It seemed that there were not enough hours in the day to see all the sights. Mick promised her that they would come back again and spend at least a full week in the capital, and maybe a few days to visit Stratford-on-Avon and the Cotswolds.

Mick waited until nine o'clock on the Monday to make sure that the solicitors would be open.

When the receptionist answered the call he asked for Mr Hodgson and was put thought immediately.

"Hodgson speaking, how can I help you?"

"My name is Michael Furford; I am led to believe that you acted on behalf of Sir George Draycot in the matter of his will."

"Yes, that is correct."

"I have been told that I am a beneficiary of that will. Sir George was my father."

"Mr Furford may I ask where you lived as a child?"

"Yes. I lived with my mother and adoptive father in Wolverhampton."

"I see, well that corresponds with the information I have, but I would need to see proof, some sort of identification. Can you arrange to call and see me?"

"That's no problem, but I live in France and am only here for a few days. Could I call tomorrow as I fly back on Wednesday? I'm staying in London so could be with you about midday."

"Shall we say twelve o'clock then? You have my address I take it?"

"Yes. Twelve o'clock is fine. Good day."

He replaced the phone and looked at Giselle.

"Do you want to come with me or would you prefer to have a day shopping?"

Her grin was all the answer he needed.

The taxi he had ordered dropped Giselle in Oxford Street on the way to the station. Shopping was not one of his favourite pastimes, especially for clothes, so he was contented that she had chosen not to join him on the trip to the solicitors.

He arrived outside the offices of Hodgson Smyth and Co at eleven forty five. He always liked to be punctual for meetings but feared that he would be in for a long wait. If Hodgson was anything like French lawyers then it would be another half an hour before they met.

A middle-aged woman took his name and rang through to Hodgson's secretary to let him know his twelve o'clock appointment had arrived.

"Would you like a cup of tea or coffee Mr Furford? His secretary says he won't be long, he's just on a call at the moment."

"Thank you, coffee, white no sugar please."

He took a seat and settled down to wait. A young girl appeared with his coffee as if by magic. The coffee was hot and surprisingly tasty, more like French coffee, not the normal insipid stuff that most English people served up. He hardly had time to finish his drink when a young lady, with her hair tied in a bun and dressed in a white blouse and grey skirt, appeared and called his name. Mick immediately took her for a secretary and stood up. She beckoned him to follow her.

Mr Hodgson sat behind a large partners' desk in a battered old leather swivel chair. The office looked like something out of a Dickens novel with numerous book shelves weighed down with leather bound books. His desk was strewn with papers and Mick wondered how on earth he could ever find anything.

The senior partner stood up and held out his hand to Mick.

"Good day, I hope you had a good journey up." He had a deep rich voice which boomed across the office.

"Yes thank you."

"May I get to the point? Sir George left most of his estate to his two daughters, but in addition he made a bequest of £500,000 to his son, born from his relationship with one Florence Cowper, whose last known address was Chester Road Wolverhampton. When Sir George died we tried to find his son, but were told that he had been reported missing in action presumed dead. There was no time limitation on the bequest and therefore can be claimed at any time, providing the claimant's credentials can be proven. Have you brought documentation with you?"

"Yes."

Mick reached into his jacket pocket and took out the papers that Giselle had brought with her. He slid them across the desk and Hodgson quickly examined them.

"They all seem to be in order, may I take a copy for my files?"

Mick nodded and the secretary was summoned to the office.

"It will take about a week if that is alright with you and then I can release the funds. I would think that the amount will be in the order of about £800,000. Quite a sum of money, which will no doubt change your life."

"I think not Mr Hodgson; I have a very successful business in France and am already very wealthy. Here is my card please have all the documents etc. sent to my office."

Mick stood up and shook the solicitor's hand.

"Goodbye and thank you."

The lady on reception rang for a taxi and, after a ten minute wait, he was on his way to the station and back to London to see what damage Giselle had done to his credit card.

CHAPTER FORTY-ONE

The visit to England had been more eventful than he could have possibly imagined. The paperwork to obtain the two inheritances had been more complicated than he first thought, and he had got his own solicitor involved to make sure everything was correct. There had been documents to sign and re-sign and it took over four weeks to finalise everything. Eventually all the money was transferred to his private account, but not before the English Government took a hefty slice to pay inheritance tax.

James had phoned a couple of times asking when Mick could come over to meet Jayne, and each time Mick had made an excuse that he was busy at work. In fact he wanted to clear all the legal business with the inheritance first.

Having finally received the net proceeds Mick felt happy to arrange his visit and rang James.

"James, hi, I was wondering if I could come over in a couple of weeks' time. It will be Easter and I assume that you will be able to take a few days off then."

"Yes, that sounds like a good idea and Nigel will be off too, so we can all meet up."

"Good, then we will fly into Heathrow and stay for the weekend. If we can meet you on Good Friday we can spend the rest of the day together, we'll catch the train up to Coventry in the morning and be with you at lunch time. How does that sound?"

"It sounds good to me. When you get to Coventry take a taxi to Broadgate, there's a statute of Lady Godiva on her horse in the middle of the traffic island, you can't miss it, we'll be waiting there."

"Fine, look forward to seeing you; give my love to your mother."

"I will... bye."

Mick put the phone down then picked it up again and dialled his solicitor.

"Henri, can you come over I have a job I need you to undertake for me." He preferred to conduct his business with Henri in his own office rather than going to him, and he had enough financial clout for Henri to comply.

Henri was there within the hour and was ushered into Mick's office.

"Michael, good morning. What is so important that I need to rush over here?"

"Henri, don't moan, you know you love to get out of the office from time to time and anyway, aren't I your most important client?"

Mick was teasing him but Henri knew he was right, Mick was his most influential client and also the best paying one.

"Henri, as you know I have recently come into a large inheritance from relations I have rediscovered in England. The papers that I asked you to look over, you remember?"

"Yes, two different legacies as I recall."

"That is correct. The net amount after U.K. taxation is £660,000. Well I want you to draw up a deed of gift covering the total amount and send it, with a cheque, to a Jayne Harris, at this address." He passed a sheet of paper to Henri with Jayne's address printed on it."

"Michael are you sure you want to do this? We are talking about a lot of money. Who is this woman anyway?"

"She's my daughter."

Henri let out a gasp of surprise.

"It happened before I left England. I knew of her birth but have never seen her. I wanted to wait until the war was over, but events overtook me and, as you know, until recently, I'd lost all recall of my previous life. Well now I know who and where she is and we are going over soon to meet her. Henri, I am a very wealthy man and the boys are well provided for. Until just a few weeks ago I knew nothing of these inheritances, so I will not miss them, and hopefully it will go some way to make up for my not looking after her all this time."

Henri nodded, he had known Mick for many years and his kindness was legendary, he understood exactly why he was doing this.

"I'll get on with it straight away, if you will arrange for the funds to be transferred to my clients' account I should be able to complete everything within a couple of days."

Mick stood up and thanked Henri. It had not been a difficult decision, especially as Giselle had been whole-hearted in her approval.

CHAPTER FORTY-TWO

When James phoned her with the news that he had met his grandfather, Jayne nearly fainted with the shock.

"But... but... are you sure? How? When? I don't understand."

"Mum just sit down and take a breath. He rang me out of the blue. I didn't believe it at first. He asked me to meet him and I went to London, he was with his wife."

"You didn't tell me."

"No, I wanted to make sure it was genuine first and he was worried that you would not want to see him."

"I'm confused, where has he been all these years? Why did he never try and find us?"

"He's lived in France since the war, married with twin boys and is a successful business man. The reason he was never in touch was that when the allies invaded France he was injured and left for dead. A French family found him and nursed him back to health, but the accident had caused him complete memory loss, which stayed with him until last Christmas, when he had severe concussion which reversed the condition. As soon as he could, he came over to look for his father and found out about my investigations. He got my number from the solicitors in Wolverhampton."

"Unbelievable!"

"Yes but it's true. I even checked with Mr Renshaw and he confirms his identity."

"So does he want to see me?"

"Yes very much so. He is coming over at Easter and I have arranged for him to meet us in the city centre, under Lady Godiva's statute on Good Friday at twelve noon."

"Is that the best you could do? What if it's raining?"

"Oh Mum, trust you to be pedantic. I thought it was a good idea for an historic meeting, Coventry's most famous historic landmark."

"Okay I give in; it's not such a bad idea."

"I told Nigel as well and he is coming down."

Jayne hung up then walked over to the drinks cabinet. It was only eleven thirty but she needed a drink. When the news finally sunk in her thoughts went to her mother. Would she want to know or would she prefer to stay ignorant? She was happily settled in her life and Granville doted on her, but if she didn't tell her and then she found out, would that break the relationship between mother and daughter?

It was after the second whisky that she made up her mind.

"Mum, it's Jayne," she said, stating the obvious. "I've just had some news which may come as a bit of a shock." Well it certainly did to me, she thought.

"What news? Has something happened to James or Nigel?"

"No nothing like that. It's not bad news. You remember in the summer James trying to trace my father?"

"Yes, I told him it was a waste of time, he died in the invasion of France."

"That's the point, he didn't. He's turned up. He lives in France and is married with two grown up boys."

"What?" Her mother almost screamed the word. "It's impossible."

"It's true; James has met him and confirmed it, he wants to come over at Easter to meet me. Do you want to meet him?"

The words hung in the air and there was a long silence before her mother replied.

"No, I don't think that would be a good idea. We have both moved on and have our own lives. Best to leave well alone, but I'm glad you told me. What intrigues me is why has he left it all these years before finding you?"

"James says that he was injured during the invasion and lost his memory and has only just got it back."

"Well at least you know that he didn't abandon you, I'm pleased about that."

Jayne put the phone down and then replaced the top back on the whisky bottle, two glasses were more than enough at lunch time or she would be asleep all afternoon.

If Jayne had been shocked by James's phone call, she was even more surprised a few days later when she opened her post. A letter addressed to her but with a French postmark was at the back of a bundle of circulars and bills. Intrigued, she ran her finger through the envelope and tore it open. The heading was a firm of solicitors in Caen, France, it read:

Dear Mrs Harris,

We are writing on behalf of our client M. M Furford who has instructed us to send you this deed of gift and a cheque in the sum of £660,000. We would be grateful if you could return the copy of the deed, enclosed, duly signed that you have safe receipt of the same.

Henri Le Grande
Partner

Jayne read the letter twice, her hands trembling as she held the cheque, she had never seen so much money in her life. Her mind was awash with questions that only her father could answer. It was a fortune, how on earth could he have so much money, let alone give it away. She opened her bureau and locked the cheque in the small drawer inside. She resolved to speak to her father before touching the money again. It was so unreal that surely it could not be true. In fact it was so surreal, perhaps the typist who had written the cheque had added too many noughts. Well, Easter was not far away and she would find out then.

CHAPTER FORTY-THREE

The plane touched down on the Heathrow tarmac. It was only a short flight between the capitals, and the attendants had barely time to serve drinks before the 'fasten seat belts' sign had come on. Mick had drunk a large brandy, he needed it. For the last week he had been anticipating the meeting with Jayne, wondering how she would react, how he would react. It had been a long time and although they were connected by blood they were strangers. As always, Giselle had been her sympathetic reassuring self, telling him that everything would be fine and it would be a happy occasion. If he would only relax!

They cleared customs and took a taxi to Claridges; having enjoyed their last stay there it had been the obvious choice. It was late afternoon by the time they checked in; Mick had decided to fly over on the Thursday, so that they would be refreshed for the journey to Coventry in the morning.

For a change Mick had pre-booked dinner at the Savoy Grill, he had read somewhere that many celebrities, both from the entertainment world and politicians, often dined there and hoped to spot some famous faces.

Having unpacked, showered and changed they took a taxi to the Savoy. He was pleased to see that there was a strict dress code, and any man who was not wearing a tie was either refused entry or offered a house tie to put on. They were escorted to a seat by the window where they could see everyone entering, not only the hotel but also the Savoy theatre opposite.

The meal was superb and the selection of wines vast. Mick did not smoke himself but loved the aroma of fine cigars. Fortunately, a man at the next table was providing him with the second-hand pleasure that emanated from the large Havana he was smoking. They drank their brandies and for the first time that day he felt relaxed, perhaps tomorrow wouldn't be so traumatic after all. It was still fairly early when they finished their meal, so they went into the foyer and turned left towards the American Bar. The sound of a piano playing a jazz classic wafted towards them. The American Bar was renowned as one of the city's premier cocktail bars and was bustling with activity. The pianist was labouring against a tide of constant chatter but somehow managing to be heard above it all. The waiter brought a menu of cocktails. Mick settled for a Rusty Nail and Giselle a Gin Sling. She squeezed his hand as if to say 'it will be okay' and he smiled back and nodded.

They stopped for another round of drinks before returning to the foyer and asking the doorman to hail a taxi. Mick wanted to be fresh for the morning, and certainly did not want to meet his daughter for the first time suffering from a hangover.

They were up and had finished breakfast by half past eight. They were catching the ten twenty train from Euston and Mick hated rushing, so wanted to make sure that he was at the station in good time. It was only about ten minutes by taxi to the station, but Mick wanted to be there at least half an hour before departure, to make sure he had time to buy the tickets and find the correct platform.

Giselle smiled to herself, he had always been like this; he would never be rushed and would rather be ten minutes early than one minute late. It was a trait that was endearing, though could sometimes be irritating as well.

They duly arrived at the terminus and having purchased their tickets settled down to wait for the announcement that the train could be boarded.

The announcer's voice boomed out across the concourse.

"The train for Coventry, Birmingham New Street and Wolverhampton is now available for boarding on platform two."

They walked to the gate leading to the train as the voice repeated the call.

The journey was uneventful; Mick passed the time reading a magazine he had brought at the newsagent's, while Giselle watched as the fields rushed past the window. The day was overcast though thankfully not raining, a typical English spring day in fact!

Arriving in Coventry, it did not take long to cross the bridge over the lines to the exit, where a long line of cabs were waiting for the exodus of passengers. With no luggage to slow them down they were the first to the rank, and were soon being whisked away towards their destination in Broadgate.

The cabby pulled up and Mick settled the fare with a tip that was as much as the cost of the journey. They got out and looked around to get their bearings. They had been dropped at the top of 'The Precinct', a pedestrian only area with shops on either side. As they faced this mall with the square behind them, on the right at the end of some shops stood The Hotel Leofric, and at right angles a large department store called Owen Owen forming one side of the square. To their left were more shops, and at right angles to these there was a building, which had obviously once been a bridge, but was now built under, with a large clock face. As they looked the clock struck noon and under the face, to the left, a door opened and a model figure of a woman on a horse slowly moved around a small balcony, returning through a door on the right. Lady Godiva appearing before the people of Coventry again. The clock building formed the opposite side of the square to the Owen Owen building.

Mick took the scene in before turning round to face the green square, which formed an island in the middle of the busy city traffic. Standing in the centre of the island was a large white plinth with a bronze statue of a naked woman sitting side saddle on a white horse, her modesty protected by long flowing hair.

Under the statue he could see three people, a woman and two young men. One of the men was waving to catch his attention, and as soon as Mick saw him he stepped off the kerb to run across to him. The motor cyclist had no chance to swerve. Giselle let out a blood curdling scream, as the figures under the statue ran forward.

Tears streaming down her face Jayne stood looking at the scene in horror. She had seen her father but never met him.

EPILOGUE

The church of Eglise St. Etienne was full to overflowing, there were even people standing on the pavement outside. The twins had shut all the showrooms and workshops of Remich Motors Ltd for three days of mourning, and it seemed as if every employee had made the journey to Caen to pay their last respects. Even the mayor of the city was there. He asked if he could say a few words about the man who was universally liked and respected, and who had done so much for the local community.

Giselle had insisted that Jayne, James and Nigel should stay at her house while they attended the funeral, after all they were part of Mick's family. She had even obtained a mantilla for Jayne, who not being a Catholic, was not aware of the protocol. James and Nigel had purchased dark suits and black ties, for this sadly, was the first funeral that they had ever attended.

After the Mass and the internment the family and a few specially invited friends returned to the house for refreshments. Jayne felt alone, desolate. She had been so happy on that fateful morning, looking forward to meeting her father and getting to know him, making up for all those lost years and now at the last moment that had been snatched from her. Here in France, in a strange house, surrounded by people she did not know, with only James and Nigel for comfort, she had never felt so desperate.

She sat quietly in the corner, away from the hubbub and sobbed, her lost father lost for ever.